Counting Crows

Poppy Reese

Pot of Potatoes Publishing

The characters and events portrayed in this book are fictitious. Any similarity to real persons, living or dead, is coincidental and not intended by the author.

ISBN-13: 979-8-9939044-0-5

Cover design by: Poppy Reese
Library of Congress Control Number:
Pot of Potatoes Publishing
Printed in the United States of America

Dedicated to Grandmama,
Without whom this mystery would have remained a mystery.

Counting Crows

By Poppy Reese

Chapter One:

There is something unsettling about a night without stars. It is the dark pause, the loss of familiarity, the subtle feeling that the universe has turned its gaze away from something so incredibly amiss.

A man with reddish brown hair covered by a tan fedora that tastefully matched his overcoat ground a cigarette out on the sidewalk with the heel of his shoe and sighed.

Agent Arnold Abberline had been trying to enjoy his fall holiday quietly with his family, though he supposed that wasn't possible for someone of his position.

He had parked a block away so that he could walk to the crime scene to clear his head. The night was cold, and a crisp wind nipped at his neck and face as he made his way towards the apartment complex.

There were at least three police cars, their lights flashing red and blue, blinding in the darkness of the night. There was an ambulance there as well, though he doubted it would be of any use now.

He stepped across the caution tape that bordered the growing mass of spectators pressing in and around the scene. There was a body lying on the ground in the middle of the alleyway. Blood had splattered on the ground beneath the body like some sick Jackson Pollock.

It was that of a woman. She had long blonde hair that was thick with blood. Her blue eyes stared vacantly up at the dark sky. Her skin was white from the bloodloss, and her lips were blue. She wore a gray V-necked sweater over a dress that had once been white. Her throat had been cut, and she was noticeably missing the ring finger on her left hand.

Out of the corner of his eye he noticed the chief-of-police standing and talking with one of her detectives as the milieu of officers, forensics specialists, and the coroner busied themselves about her. She was only a little younger than the director and had a matronly disposition, a blonde bob and brown eyes that seemed stern and kind all at the same time. Slipping his hands in his pockets, he strolled over to her.

"Oh, hi. Glad you could make it," Chief Carol Abberline said, pecking her husband on the cheek. "Did the babysitter get there alright?"

"She got there fine. Only a few minutes after you left. What's all this?"

"It's the Richmond Ripper's signature," the chief remarked, nodding at the corpse.

"That's the third in the last four months," Agent Abberline said.

"And right when we thought he might have quieted down again."

"Maybe if that Crestmont woman would quit writing those obscene articles on him, he wouldn't keep resurfacing. It's like she's challenging him."

"That's just her way. Egging on murderers with both insult and encouragement."

"How many victims now?" the director asked, nodding at the body.

"Well, there's the one in Richmond, Virginia, ten years ago with three victims. Then he reappeared sporadically. He took two in Massachusetts, one in Maryland, three in California, one in Nevada, then all the way back here...so about fourteen victims including her."

Agent Abberline shook his head.

"What about Vale? Have you called her to come in for the profiling yet?"

"Not yet, no. I'll call her as soon as we get back to tell her about this new development; we'll need her input on it as well."

"Was she able to identify anything that might trigger these murders?"

"No, we still only know as much as we knew before."

Their conversation was broken by Head-detective Alastor Creed, a tall man with jet black hair which was graying far too early for a man in his mid-thirties. He too wore a gray fedora and a matching gray trench coat. His face was sharp and stern with slight wrinkles around his brow, forehead, and eyes from his steady frown. He had a prominent nose and hard, colorless eyes. He tipped his hat to the chief and the agent upon reaching them.

"Oh, good evening, Agent," he said, noticing Abberline, then turning to the chief, "forensics confirmed that the woman's throat was slit most likely by a hunting knife. Other than that, though, they have no other information."

"No trace of the Ripper at all?" the chief asked, her face hardening.

"None. No fingerprints, no DNA, nothing," Det. Creed remarked.

"Were there any witnesses?"

"Only the old lady that called in, the one that heard the screams from the second floor. Apparently, the woman lived in this apartment, was on her way home, and then he attacked. The strange part is that she didn't seem to fight back. There are no defense wounds."

"Maybe he was waiting for her. He could have been waiting in that alley there, jumped out and surprised her and killed her before she could do anything," Agent Abberline suggested, taking out another cigarette from his coat pocket and lighting it.

"That's not what happened at all. The woman clearly knew him personally, at least by acquaintance. Thus she didn't put up a fight. You should go through her phone. They probably corresponded through text or call."

Agent Abberline, Chief Abberline, and Det. Creed turned around to look at who had spoken. In the front of the crowd that had gathered around the caution tape, having pushed her way to the front to watch in meek interest, was a girl around sixteen years old. She had a pleasant, pale, oval face surrounded by heavily sprayed, short hair and fringe the same color as a pearl, decorated with intricate bobby pins. She had a button nose and full lips pressed firmly together in a pensive frown. Her eyes were the color of a periwinkle flower, wide and intense. She wore a white button down, a baby blue sweater, a trench coat, and a plaid skirt, white leg warmers, gloves, blue slippers and carried with her a brown satchel covered in pins depicting emblems of musicians such as The Smiths or Blondie or more simple ones such as frogs or butterflies.

She had an interesting manner of speaking as well, Agent Abberline noticed. Though not too prominent, she sounded as though she had come from a black and white movie out of the 1940s. He noticed also that she seemed to be copying their own characteristics and vocalizations, however unintentionally.

"What did you say?" Det. Creed asked.

"I said they clearly knew each other. They had to have kept in contact somehow, so you ought to check her phone," the girl repeated, lifting the caution tape and making her way underneath to closer inspect the crime scene despite the incredulous looks of the agent, chief, and detective.

"Why didn't anyone think to do that yet?" Chief Abberline asked after a moment, looking pointedly at Creed.

"I'll have someone check her contacts at once, ma'am," Det. Creed replied, scurrying off to talk to forensics, who had collected all the woman's things for evidence.

"So...what do *you* think happened to her then?" Agent Abberline asked the strange girl, watching her curiously.

She didn't seem to hear the question, for she was pondering the body quite keenly, so the man tapped her on the shoulder. The girl brushed his hand away and looked around at him and he repeated his question.

"The killer is a man, I believe the Richmond Ripper, if I'm not mistaken."

"That's right," the chief nodded.

"They had known each other, as I said before, and long enough for him to gain her trust. He was with her at the time; they were out together...a date perhaps...thus, why she's dressed so nicely. I'd say an Italian restaurant discerning from the oregano on her sweater. They might even be able to describe the man she was with to you, and, henceforth, your killer. Further, she didn't even see it coming. They're chatting, probably having a good time. He falls behind her, she doesn't notice. Then he grabbed her and slit her throat before she could even think to defend herself. She flopped around a little bit; you can obviously tell that from the way the blood splattered on the ground and walls; though it's only on this one because she was too weak to struggle much. He drops her to the ground, cuts off her finger there. He lets her bleed to death, but he's gone before she's dead. Then the old lady called in. "

"How on earth did a kid figure all that out?" Agent Abberline asked.

"It's simple deduction and perception. 'Elementary, Watson' and so on and so on. You see, I get the feeling he killed her with purpose. It would explain the ring finger being cut off. It's so simple...it's the finger you wear the wedding ring on. Maybe he's only going after a certain type of girl, for revenge, or justice, or love, or whatever it is in his sick mind. One thing's for certain: he meant to take her finger. That's his trophy, his signature."

"My detectives must be dull if they couldn't pull all that together as quickly as you did," Chief Abberline remarked, her eyebrows raised in amusement. "Det. Creed, tell the officers to check out all the Italian restaurants within walking distances. Show them this woman's picture and ask if she was with anyone."

"Right away," Det. Creed answered.

"You've got a pretty useful talent, kid," Agent Abberline remarked. "That is, unless you did it."

"What do you mean?" the girl asked in confusion.

"How do we know that you weren't a witness or even an accomplice to this crime and *that's* really how you know all this?"

"Arnold—"

"No, really think about it, Carol. She just told me *exactly* what the killer did and why. I think she knows more than you let on."

"I told you, I just analyzed the situation—"

"Maybe I should bring you in. At least for a witness report," Chief Abberline agreed.

"Hold on," the girl said, beginning to back away. "I didn't do anything connected to this case."

"Maybe not, but you're still coming with us—"

When Agent Abberline reached out to take the girl by the shoulder, she had brushed his hand away, and attempted to run. Of course, the director was fast and caught the girl by the arm. What he didn't expect was for the girl to retaliate by kicking him in the ankle and kneeing him in the stomach before fleeing the crime scene much faster than he had thought her capable.

❀❀❀

"She definitely knows something," the director grunted, as his wife hurried to check on him.

"It seems that way," the chief agreed, helping him to his feet.

"Arnold, are you alright?" Det. Creed asked, hurrying over.

"Catch that kid," Agent Abberline told him.

"She headed towards downtown," the detective remarked.

"Alastor, you and Arnold take your cars and head her off. I'll stay here and monitor the crime scene," the chief ordered.

"On it," Creed said.

They hurried in opposite directions to where their cars were parked, and, hopping inside, started the engines, pulling away from the sidewalk. Creed went one way, and Abberline the other with the idea that one would catch the girl, and the other would block her attempted escape.

Abberline made his way downtown faster than the speed limit allowed, though he felt that, under the current circumstances and the fact that he was the director of the BAU for the FBI, it would be excused.

Agent Abberline drove around until he came to the bad part of town where everything was rather run-down and dingy. He knew the girl had to be around here somewhere seeing as how she only got less than a five minute head start.

As he was passing a red brick apartment building that seemed better off demolished, he noticed a figure running down the dark alley between the apartment building and the house next to it. He slammed on his brakes at once and U-turned in the middle of the street. He pulled back around just in time to see the girl climbing up the fire escape on the side of the building, unaware of her pursuer, and disappearing through the window of an apartment on the seventh floor.

He pulled his car into the parking lot of the building and went inside. The lobby was just like the outside with old, stained carpeting, peeling, yellowed wallpaper, and reeking of dank and smoke. A thin, lanky young man with wild, curly hair pulled back in a ponytail and an unshaven face who looked like the human embodiment of the building sat, slumped over the front desk, stoned.

"Excuse me," Agent Abberline said to him. "Excuse me!"

"Huh?" the young man grunted, looking up at him with red, puffy eyes.

"Did you see a girl around sixteen come through here? Or in this building at all for that matter?"

"Man, I don't know nobody here. I just work the desk. Keep my head low," the man drawled.

"Can you at least tell me what room a certain person lives in?" the director asked irritatedly.

"No way, man. I don't even know who you are."

Sighing impatiently, Agent Abberline extracted his badge and held it out for the young man to see. The young man's eyes widened in shock.

"Look, man, I don't know nuthin' about nuthin', 'kay?" he remarked nervously, raising his hands.

"I need to know if there's a blonde, blue eyed girl, about this tall living in this building, or I'll run you in for a list of charges, including whatever the hell you're smoking," the director growled, jabbing a finger in the young man's face.

"There's only one *girl* who lives here. Room 713."

Abberline took the elevator to the seventh floor. Apparently, the seventh floor was deserted. Most of the apartment doors were open, some locked and caution taped, some awaiting new tenants. He found room 713 and put his ear to the door. He could hear a rustling coming from inside. He knocked and listened again. The room had fallen silent inside.

He frowned, rapping on the door again but still received no answer. He thought for a moment before he bent down to work on the lock with a pick set from his wallet. A moment later there was a click and he pushed the door open.

When he looked into the apartment he found that it was empty but for the furniture supplied. Mold was growing from the ceiling, down the peeling blue wallpaper, and behind the tatty couch. The small sink by the kitchenette was leaking, and the window was cracked and broken, mended with silver duct tape. He could see into the open door of the bedroom and saw that it was no better than the rest of the apartment, but was cluttered with books, notebooks, papers and clothes strewn and stacked around. But the girl was nowhere in sight.

He noticed that there was another window in the bedroom and crossed the threshold to search the room more closely. Inspecting the window, he found that the lock was undone and lifting it, he looked out. He saw that there was a fire escape below, which had recently been pulled down in order to be used.

"Great," the director sighed.

❀❀❀

Det. Creed was sitting in his car, watching the streets for any sign of their quarry when his phone rang. He saw that it was Agent Abberline and answered.

"She got away," Abberline remarked. "Crawled down the fire escape. She might be headed your way. Keep an eye out."

"This is so ridiculous—"

Det. Creed paused in his sentence to watch as the girl from the crime scene ran down the sidewalk next to him, her hair flying wildly about her face and what looked to be a cat in her arms.

"Alastor, are you there?"

"Found her," Creed said.

He ran his car across the street and swerved up onto the sidewalk so she couldn't get past. She tried turning to run the other way but was blinded by the headlights of Agent Abberline's car.

"I don't have anything to do with that murder!" she cried, as she watched the director exit his car.

"Then why did you run?" Agent Abberline replied.

"Rookie mistake. But still, it's none of your business."

"And where do you think you were going, jumping out a window?" he asked.

"I don't know, actually," she admitted. "I just didn't want to get arrested. That's the last thing I need right now."

"All of this sounds really suspicious, you know."

"I know," the girl sighed, staring through Abberline.

I'm still going to have to bring you down to the station for questioning."

"But—"

"I would recommend you come quietly, young lady. If nothing else, you're a witness. It's just a few questions to make sure you aren't involved and a witness report."

The girl reluctantly followed Agent Abberline to his car. Just then, the thing in the girl's arms meowed and the agent looked down to see the ugliest cat, that is, if it was a cat, he had ever seen. Its white fur stuck out in all directions and grayed on the ends; its teeth protruded from its mouth so that its tongue stuck out and its crossed eyes bulged from their sockets.

"Is that a cat?" he asked.

"Her name's Magnolia," the girl replied.

"Great, now I'm gonna have cat fur in my car."

Chapter Two:

Cosette, still holding the hideous cat, sat in the chair on one side of the interrogation table.

"Christ, that thing was a cat?" Creed said in surprise, recognising the animal as he sat down opposite the girl.

"Now, this is just for the record," Abberline said, "to clear you as a suspect. Okay?"

The girl didn't answer and only frowned at them indignantly.

"What's your name?"

"Cosette H. Bordeaux—the 'H' is for Helenor."

"Wait, *you're* Cosette Bordeaux?" Det. Creed asked incredulously.

"Yes," the girl nodded.

"The writer for the *Virginia Times*?"

"Yes."

"Can I speak to you for a moment, Arnold?"

"Yes, of course."

He followed Creed out of the interrogation room to the observation room and waited while the head-detective went to the file room and searched through the filing cabinets and returned holding a thin manilla file and his laptop. He slammed the folder down on the table with a little more force than necessary.

"What is that?" Agent Abberline asked curiously.

"The chief tells you about all the cases from work, right?"

"A good deal of them."

"So, you know about the time the Best Buy on Koger Center Boulevard was robbed by that petty thief?"

"Yes, Carol said someone called in and told them exactly how the store was robbed and even pointed out one of the robbers in the crowd saying that he was continuously nervous ticking and had been standing outside the store for two days. They knew this because the Best Buy had been on another news channel a couple days before and they had seen the robber in the background. We checked it out and found out that he had dropped his phone while making a break for it after the robbery and had been attempting to figure out how to get it without the cops spotting him."

"And what about the time that woman got kidnapped from the Fan District?"

"They found the woman within two and a half days of her kidnapping because they discovered her dog in the woods."

"Wrong," Creed said. "An unknown caller found the dog in the woods, traced it back from where it had come from, found the kidnapper's house and called in."

"So? An anonymous person calls in every now and then with a tip, so what?" Abberline asked.

"The person brought the dog into one of our officers. The officer described the caller as 'a nice, blonde teenage girl'."

Abberline looked through the double-sided mirror at Cosette, who was wandering about the interrogation room.

"A few weeks ago, when Janice Roland was murdered by her ex-boyfriend, the anonymous caller was at the crime scene. She pointed out that it wasn't a suicide like everyone thought, that asphyxiation by rope looked different than that by hands, that there were defense wounds, and also remarked that her lock was scratched like it had been picked. Well, when the officer asked her what her name was, she said it was '*Cosette H. Bordeaux —'H' for Helenor.*' I had put together a file of all the times this 'Caller' called and they're all from *Cosette H. Bordeaux.*"

"Well, I suppose it's worth asking her about—huh?"

"What? Whoa!" Creed jumped back, having followed Abberline's gaze to the double-sided mirror.

The girl was standing only a few inches away from the glass, staring through it as if she could see them, ignoring the weird cat as it licked the glass.

"Can she see us?" Det. Creed asked.

"I don't think so," Abberline replied uncertainly.

They stood there momentarily, Creed moving his hand to and fro in front of the glass to test if the girl could really see them through it, though they were both unsettled when her eyes seemed to follow his movements.

"Let's just...get back to the task at hand," Abberline said uncomfortably and they returned to the interrogation room, sitting opposite her again.

"So you do this often?" he asked Cosette, sliding the Manilla file to her.

"I can't help that I notice things like this. I don't know how it happens; perhaps it comes with being a writer, I suppose," the girl replied stiffly, as she looked through the file.

"Or—and here's a crazy yet plausible thought—are you connected to all the cases?" Det. Creed growled, pointing a finger in between her eyes.

"Oh, again with this. Yeah, I helped rob the Best Buy, kidnapped that lady, *and* killed Janice Roland," Cosette said snarkily.

"Is that a confession?" Det. Creed asked, resting his weight on his palm.

"No, Shotgun, it's not," Cosette replied, eying him irritatedly.

"So, she has tipped off the police more than once, I think that serves her case rather well actually, don't you?" Abberline remarked to the head-detective. "We have proof that this is just a...strange hobby of hers."

Det. Creed growled.

"So shall we continue the interrogation?"

"Yes, if you would," Cosette said.

"What is your age?"

"Sixteen."

"Birthdate?"

"February 7, 2008."

"We know where you live, so...Who are your parents?"

"Angeline and Albert Bordeaux."

"And where are they at the moment?"

"They currently reside in Green Mount Cemetery in Baltimore, Maryland."

"Why is that?"

"Because they're dead. It's no wonder you can't solve cases," Cosette returned.

Creed scowled at her remark, beginning to open his mouth, but Abberline jumped in before he could say anything.

"How long?"

"Nine years."

"My condolences. You must live with relatives now then?

"No, I live alone."

"Since you were seven?" Det. Creed asked skeptically. "Yeah, I don't think so. Now I certainly think you're lying."

"I ran away. A year ago."

"Oh good, one of *those*," Creed grumbled.

"Like you're a bowl of ice cream," Cosette snapped back.

"Why did you run away?" Agent Abberline asked, before conflict could ensue between the two.

"Because my relatives were a pain in the ass."

"Oh, of course," Abberline nodded. "How about this, how did you know all that about the victim tonight?"

"Like I said before, I'm a writer of murder and mystery, you have to know these things. I sell my short stories to the *Virginia Times*, not unlike Dickens, and have even published a book. Some of them are even based on real happenings and things I've solved myself. You can look me up. I have an alibi," she said, straightening in her chair.

"She does," Creed agreed irritatedly, drumming his fingers on his crossed arms.

"Besides I thought we all agreed the Richmond Ripper did this," Cosette said suddenly.

"What were you doing out at this time of night anyway?"

"Jimmy was smoking weed at the front desk, and I could smell it up in my apartment. I was getting a headache and decided to go out for supper and a walk. On my way back, I saw the crime scene and thought it might make for a good story. Of course, those plans were interestingly disrupted—and frankly, I don't know whether to be annoyed or pleased."

"Yes, our apologies. As we *have* all agreed, it was surely the Richmond Ripper. We're just following protocol. We'll check the security cameras at the places you've said you've been. Where did you eat tonight?"

"The Chinese buffet a block from the crime scene. And that was around eight o' clock."

"Okay. I don't think you had anything to do with this except wrong place wrong time,

Abberline said. "Or perhaps the right time since we may now have gained some leads from it. Can we just get forensics to take a couple DNA samples and have you put in a report now, just in case?"

"Sure," Cosette agreed, nodding.

"Oh, and can I have the number of someone trusted, just for reference?"

"I don't know her number, but you can look her up. Dr. Adlea Vale. I think she's with the University of Virginia now."

"You know Vale?" Abberline asked.

"Yes, she was my psychologist when I was younger. Why?"

"Oh, it's nothing. We're just acquainted as well."

"Oh, well, perhaps she'll be able to persuade you that I'm not an accessory to a serial killer," Cosette said, standing up and rolling her joints so that they cracked.

"I'm sure we're already convinced of your innocence, Miss Bordeaux."

"I'm not," Creed muttered.

"Hush, Alastor," the director hissed. "Thank you for your

cooperation. Oh, and Det. Creed, please escort Miss Bordeaux to the forensics lab."

"Yes, sir," Creed said.

He took Cosette by the arm, but she jerked roughly away.

"I can walk on my own, thank you," she growled, glaring at the detective and adjusting her coat.

"You're a delight, aren't you?" Det. Creed snapped.

"Only as much as yourself," the girl replied.

Agent Abberline chuckled to himself when they had gone. Then he thought to himself. The girl obviously had nothing to do with the murder, so she was simply talented. The kind of talented the police and even the FBI could use. She had noticed things that probably would have taken the detectives days to notice just by looking at the body.

He was curious about her though. He decided to borrow his wife's office while it was vacant and make a few calls. Just as he was making his way across the stations, he heard his name being called by the last person he wanted to see right then.

Pandora Crestmont was beautiful and that was exactly how she managed to get her nose into things that would likely get it cut off. Most people expected a sleazy tableau reporter to be some greased up old man who smelled like smoke and cheap cologne, not a gorgeous woman with neat, shiny black hair, sparkling blue eyes, and a slim figure. Still, Pandora Crestmont could talk her way in and out of anything as well as she could twist her words and cheat people out of their reputations.

She was often tailed by her cameraman, an awkward, lanky young man with sandy hair, a pale, freckled face and gray eyes named Conrad Finnigan. He was a transfer student from Dublin, Ireland, who was working towards a photography degree, although he was hardly as clever as Pandora.

The duo were being held back by a junior detective with messy black hair and black eyes.

"Agent Abberline! Agent Abberline! A few comments, please?" Pandora called out innocently, waving her recorder in the air.

"Seymour, how did they get in? I thought Carol specifically banned their entry," Abberline asked wearily.

"Lesly at the front desk let them in. She said Pandora scared her. Sorry, sir," Seymour said. "I'm just escorting them out now—"

Seymour was cut off by Ms. Crestmont pushing him off of them by his face.

"Agent Abberline, would you like to make any comments on the murder of Emma Alfreds? Who do you think killed her? Do you think it was the Richmond Ripper? What evidence do you have, especially backing that theory? And is the return of such a notorious killer the reason the FBI has gotten involved?"

Abberline got very close to the recorder she held out to him and then said, very clearly, "No comments. Stop annoying me."

"But, Agent Abberline—"

"But nothing, Ms. Crestmont. The details of Emma Alfreds' murder are completely confidential until further notice. Especially to you and the Exposé."

"But—!"

"Now, you and your cameraman can exit the premises, or I will personally put you in a cell."

Pandora glared hatefully at Agent Abberline, but turned on her heel making for the door, followed by Conrad. She stopped at the door and looked over her shoulder at Abberline.

"I'll have my story, one way or another," she remarked coolly before exiting the police station.

Agent Abberline shook his head and sighed.

He knew she would have her story. She always did.

Chapter Three:

Agent Abberline sat down at Chief Abberline's currently vacant desk, extracted his phone and dialed Dr. Adlea Vale's number. It was strange that Cosette had known Dr. Vale. He supposed he could kill two birds with one stone and call her about Cosette and the Ripper. Dr. Vale had been assisting them as a behavioral analyst and criminal profiler since the first time the Richmond Ripper had struck.

Dr. Vale was glad to hear from him again. She was eager to hear what he had to say about the case.

"What brings you to call at this time of night, Arnold?" Dr. Vale asked.

"I didn't wake you, did I?" Abberline asked.

"Not at all. But how can I help you?"

"Well, there are two things. First, I was wondering if you could tell me about an old patient of yours, Cosette Bordeaux?"

"Cosette," Dr. Vale mused thoughtfully. "I remember Cosette! She isn't in any trouble?"

"No, I simply wanted to clear her as a witness to a recent murder. You know, just hear from some people who knew her about her claims."

"Oh, dear, I see. Well, I haven't seen her since she was seven, and then there's the doctor-patient confidentiality, so I don't know how much help I will be on that matter."

"What *can* you tell me about her?"

"She stopped coming to me after her parents' deaths," Dr. Vale remarked.

"And do you know why?" Agent Abberline asked.

"I'm not really sure. When she moved in with her aunt and uncle, they called and said she wouldn't be taking sessions with me anymore, and that was that."

"Do you still have her aunt's or uncle's numbers? I think I ought to call them about her, but Cosette never gave their information."

"Oh, yes, I think I still have them somewhere. Give me a second."

Dr. Vale was gone for a minute before she got back and read off the phone numbers to him.

"I do hope she'll be alright," Dr. Vale said.

"Oh, she will. Now, you couldn't tell me Cosette's diagnosis, could you?"

"Not without a warrant, no," Dr. Vale responded. "I can say, though, that she always had an active imagination and was extremely creative even for a child."

"And is that why she can do the 'thing'?"

"What 'thing'?"

"Where she seems to be able to tell what people have done and why?"

"Ah, yes, that's something she's done as long as I've known her."

"It is a very useful talent she has," Agent Abberline remarked.

"I suppose you could say that," Dr. Vale agreed. "But I think that's about all I can tell you about her without breaking confidence. Is there anything else I can help you with?"

"Yes."

"What is it?"

"The Richmond Ripper is back."

"Oh, no," Dr. Vale said in concern. Then after a pause, "What is this? The third timein four months?"

"Yes, it is."

"And same as always? A girl, blonde, blue-eyed, around twenty?"

"Yes. He slit her throat, cut off her ring finger. Same pattern as always. Although there weren't any signs to say what triggered his killing again, or why. We'll require your assistance with the behavioral department again."

"Of course. I'd be happy to help. Would you like me to come in tomorrow?"

"Ah, yes, I would appreciate it if you would. We'll tell you more at the station."

"Alright then. Good night, Agent Abberline. See you tomorrow."

❀❀❀

The next morning, Aberline dialed one of the two numbers that Dr. Vale had given him. The tone rang five times before someone finally picked up.

"Who is this?' asked the harsh voice of a woman. "I'll call the cops if you're some sort of scammer!"

"My name is Agent Arnold Abberline, director of the Behavioral Analysis Unit with the FBI," he replied.

"Oh...oh my goodness. The FBI? Wh-what do we have to do with any of that?"

"Honey, who's on the phone?" came the voice of a man in the background.

"The FBI, dear."

"The what—! Put it on speaker," the man said sharply. "Who is this?"

"Agent Abberline."

"And why are you calling?"

"Are you Clarice and Quinten Fernsby?"

"We are," replied the man. "What does it mean to the FBI?"

"I'd like to ask you some questions about your niece, Cossette Bordeaux."

"We don't have a niece by that name," Mrs. Fernsby said quickly.

Abberline only took a moment in pulling up the girl's family history on his wife's work computer and the Fernsby's were the first people that showed up after her parents.

"Here it says you're the older sister of her biological mother, Mrs. Angeline Bordeaux."

From the other end of the phone there was the sound of indignant spluttering that sounded very much like a fish out of water.

"Fine, she is our niece, but we don't have anything to do with her. We haven't even seen her in a year."

"And why haven't you seen her in that long? According to her file, you're her closest relatives," Abberline asked, though he already knew the answer.

"She ran away," Mrs. Fernsby stated.

"Why do you think she would do that?"

"Heaven knows! She was a difficult and dangerously troubled child. She was just plain..."

"Strange," Mr. Fernsby assisted her.

"Yes, strange. She always seemed to know everything about everyone, even though she was so isolated from people—her own decision, of course, she never did like people. I swear, she had sociopathic tendencies. She would get violently emotional, refuse to leave the house or even eat anything. She even quit going to school. We tried to get her help, we really did, but she didn't want it," Mrs. Fernsby said. "Then one night, she just got up and ran away. We thought she must have killed herself or something, though we never heard about it on the news."

"And you never bothered to look for her or file a missing persons report?"

"Well, we *did* report her missing but it was never really prioritized."

"And where do you live currently?" the director asked.

"Vermont, why?"

"Just curious how much distance she put between you and herself."

"What do you mean?"

"She's all the way in Virginia now. She must have been awfully desperate to get away from you."

Mrs. Fernsby only exhaled hard out of her nose.

"You know, I get the strange feeling that you don't mind that she's gone," Agent Abberline said. "Perhaps you aren't telling me the whole truth here. Dr. Vale spoke kindly of her, the opposite of yourselves, and seeing as I have known Dr. Vale longer than the two of you, I feel inclined to believe *her* story."

"Well, she always did put on façades around the company," Mrs. Fernsby spat.

"I don't believe she ran away, Mr. and Mrs. Fernsby. If I may say, I believe you kicked her out."

"Outrageous!" Mrs. Fernsby cried furiously. "Why have you even called us? What do we have to do with the FBI?"

"We believed Cosette to be a witness to or was connected to a murder. It is only routine that we contact their guardians or family for certainty."

"Oh, God, I always knew she would get wrapped up in murder again," Mrs. Fernsby groaned.

"Again?"

"Cosette killed someone."

Agent Abberline stopped, faintly surprised.

"What happened?"

"Apparently, some man attacked her, and she stabbed him to death. The police found her after a while and brought her home, though she wasn't arrested. Rather, they called her a *hero* —apparently the man had been some sort of killer. Of course, we wouldn't let her identity out. Think of the shame..."

"It wasn't the Northeast Nightmare, was it?" Agent Abberline asked.

"Yes, it was."

"I was involved in that case. And I'm supposing that is why you kicked her out?"

"That's quite enough," Mr. Fernsby said suddenly. "Good evening to you, sir and don't call us again."

The man hung up and Agent Abberline sighed, shaking his

head.

"Lovely people," he muttered as the office door opened.

He turned to see his wife enter, carrying paperwork.

"Hey, honey, we just got the crime scene cleared," she said, setting the files down on her desk.

"The girl's name was Emma Alfreds. We're going to contact her family tomorrow."

"Oh, I know about that. Pandora Crestmont told me all about it," Agent Abberline grumbled.

"How did she get in?" the chief asked with a frown. "I thought I specifically said she wasn't allowed on the premises."

"I think we need to give Lesly a gun license so she can take care of Pandora the next time she tries to get past the front desk," the director chuckled.

"Oh, don't say things like that. You know Lesly couldn't bring herself to use a gun."

"If it's Pandora, she might. I know I'm tempted to," Chief Abberline chuckled. "Oh, and I did call Dr. Vale. She should be in tomorrow."

"Oh, perfect. Thank you very much for getting in contact with her," the chief said. "I still have my officers out searching for the identity of whoever Miss Alfreds was with before her death. Other than that, I say we had better get home. The babysitter's probably tired of binge watching *My Little Pony* and stepping on LEGOs."

Chapter Four:

The next morning, Agent Abberline found Creed at his desk, filing paperwork.

"Hey, how did it go with Cosette last night? Was she co-operative?"

"Yeah, but I wanted to get rid of her as soon as possible. She scared me a little. Somehow she knew about the 'Emry Incident'. I mean, not *exactly* but she was getting close and I did not want to talk about that stuff."

Agent Abberline raised his eyebrows.

"Do you remember Antony Sanguini, the Northeast Nightmare over in Vermont?"

"Yeah, it was just a year ago wasn't it?" Det. Creed asked. "Didn't his last victim stab him to death?"

"Yeah, and it was Cosette."

"Are you kidding me?"

"Apparently her aunt and uncle kicked her out afterwards and that's why she lives here on her own."

"That's heartless, even for me."

Agent Abberline nodded.

"But, at least we know she's not connected to this murder."

"We did, though, go through that victim's phone," Creed said. "We actually managed to locate the messages she's been sending the Ripper. She'd been in contact with him for about a month. Apparently they had met at some sort of book fair and had exchanged numbers to talk about books. It's mostly normal conversation and eventually they decided to go out to an Italian restaurant—that was last night, just like the brat said."

"So, no clues as to who he is? No pictures or descriptions?"

"No, nothing yet. The chief still has people out searching for descriptions and whatnot, though."

"Did forensics find anything?"

"Still nothing. It's like she was murdered by a ghost."

"After ten years of looking for this guy, I'm not so sure that isn't out of the question."

They were quiet for a moment and Agent Abberline pondered to himself for a while. The Ripper had been on the loose for ten years and no one knew the slightest thing about him. No one could find any clues as to who he was or even why he killed. The only thing anyone ever knew about him was that he had a pattern. He only killed women who looked similar, slit their throat, and cut off their ring finger, typically taking it with him.

But Cosette seemed to have gotten into his head. She had been able to tell them just what had happened.

"I'm going out," Agent Abberline remarked, taking up his jacket.

❀❀❀

Agent Abberline found himself once again at the residence—if you could even consider it a proper residence—of Cosette Bordeaux. When he knocked on her door, she opened it just wide enough to peek out without removing the chain.

"Oh, no, not you again," she groaned upon seeing him. "Here to arrest me, I suppose?"

"May I come in?" the director asked.

The girl eyed him for a moment before she stepped back to let him in.

"Excuse the mess. I never could keep anything clean. Could I offer you anything?"

Abberline declined the offer.

"Yeah, there isn't much here anyways, unless you don't

mind leftover takeout. Magnolia, get down!" the girl exclaimed suddenly.

Startled by her sudden exclamation, Abberline looked around and discovered the ugly cat Cosette owned had gotten up on top of the refrigerator and was trying to sit in a dish of sweets. She climbed up on the counter to get the cat off the fridge.

"Sorry to ask, but why did you pick a cat so ugly when there were surely others to choose from?" the director asked, watching in disgust as the girl petted the creature.

"That's exactly the reason. If I hadn't picked her, no one would have," Cosette answered. "Then the shelter would've put her down."

"Ah, I see. Now, perhaps I should tell you what I came here for?"

"Oh, yes, here, have a seat," Cosette said, and went to clear the couch of books and papers so the director could seat himself. "So, what did you come here to talk about then?"

"It is clear, after seeing what you did at the crime scene, and with all those tips you called in, that you're special. You can do things that adult detectives train years to do. And I can't let such talent go to waste. In short, I want you to help us solve the case of the Richmond Ripper," Agent Abberline remarked.

"Are you serious?" Cosette asked, clearly trying to contain excitement.

"Very much."

"Oh, yes, absolutely!" she exclaimed. "But—there will be conditions if I am to work with you, though."

"What are they?"

"I want to get paid for assisting you as a consulting detective," the girl remarked. "And I want to be able to write the cases as a mystery when we are done. I'll change names and personal information, of course. I always do."

"Fine, fair enough. But here's my condition," the director remarked in his turn. "I want to have you psychoanalyzed."

I won't be doing that," Cosette remarked stubbornly.

"Then no case."

She glared at him, crossing her arms over her chest.

"Why must I go to another psychologist?"

"Trust me, it's for your own good. I know all about the Northeast Nightmare."

Cosette froze.

"How did you find that out?" she asked, her eyes wide with fear

"You're forgetting that I'm an agent for the FBI."

"Of course, how stupid of me," the girl paused for a long beat. "I still don't need a psychologist."

"We need to make sure you're stable enough to work with us," Abberline remarked pointedly.

Cosette frowned at him.

"You know, I don't think I like you very much," she said at last. "And I'm only doing this for a novel. Tell your shrink friend I wish them luck."

❀❀❀

When the director returned to the station, he found Dr. Vale was waiting for him in the conference room. She was a pretty woman with wavy brown hair that fell a little lower than her shoulders and sparkling hazel eyes. She was slight, with full lips and a pointed nose. She wore a red button down and a black skirt, carrying with her only a red handbag.

"Hello, Dr. Vale," he greeted her. "I didn't expect you so early."

"Oh, well, my class ended early. I do have a session in a little bit though, so I only have enough time to discuss the new aspects of the case."

"Alright. Have a seat, and we'll discuss what we've found so far."

Agent Abberline went and retrieved the information they had uncovered last night, including Cosette's statement.

"So, here's what we found," Agent Abberline said, sitting down across from Dr. Vale. "As you know, the Richmond Ripper typically goes after blonde, blue-eyed young women, slits their throats and cuts off their middle finger, which is information you helped us acquire several years ago."

"And I take it that the Ripper followed this same pattern as usual?"

"Yes, exactly. But we found some new information. Apparently, the Ripper had been in contact with the victim *before* he killed her. We think this may have applied to his latter victim as well. Cosette was the one who recommended that he knew them and that we go through her phone and we actually found proof that he had been in contact with them under a false name."

"You've been in contact with Cosette?"

"Yes, we have."

"Did you ever get the chance to talk to her aunt and uncle?" Dr. Vale asked.

"Yes and they're just *charming* people," Agent Abberline replied dryly. "Oh, and I think I ought to ask if you were aware of *who* killed Antony Sanguini, the Northeast Nightmare?"

"No. I thought they kept her name confidential for privacy reasons, though the rest was in the paper."

"It was Cosette."

"What?" Vale gasped.

"Since you already know the story, I needn't retell it, but it was she who killed him. After that, her aunt and uncle kicked her out. She came to Richmond and lives alone now."

"That's awful!" Dr. Vale remarked.

"I don't think putting her in a home is the right option. From what I've seen of her, she won't go even if I try to send her. But I do want to get her a psychologist, and seeing as how you worked with her before, it might be easier for her to open up to you."

Dr. Vale sighed.

"I would love to help Cosette, I really would, but between my classes, my students, my current patients, and the Ripper resurfacing I just don't think I can."

Agent Abberline sighed.

"But you know who could take her on?" Vale asked

thoughtfully. "Dr. Carnifex."

"Oh, that is very true. He does take special and complex cases like this."

Dr. Vale nodded.

"And he's currently accepting patients. If you could set her up with him, I could send her papers over. But, to keep on track, where would you like for me to start on the case?"

"Can you look over the files I copied of the Ripper cases—past and current—and see if you see anything that could have triggered these murders again? Any behaviors or any more patterns that could lead to any more clues as to who this killer is?"

"Of course. With the phone conversations he had with Miss Alfreds, I'm sure I'll find something. I'll need the phone, though. Is it in here? Oh, good, it is—well, I'll look over it and see if there are any behavioral clues in his way of texting."

"Whatever you can find will help us. We also have asked Cosette to assist on the case due to her ability to spot things about the Ripper that we didn't. But the thing is no one would believe her in court. She's a child after all, and she isn't even in school. It could even concern our reputations. But if you're helping us as well, you can check and back up anything that Cosette might find, which would signify whatever she says, or even take full credit for it."

"Alright," Dr. Vale agreed. "But do promise me one thing."

"What is it?" the director asked.

"The Ripper is one of the most dangerous killers I've ever seen. Don't let her get too close to all of this, alright?"

"Of course not. She's just going to give us a little information on what she sees."

After giving Dr. Vale the copies of the files as well as copies of the text conversations, she left to take care of her counseling session with her patient.

When she had gone, Agent Abberline went into his phone contacts and found the one labeled "Dr. Carnifex" and rang him.

"Hello, Arnold," a calm voice answered. "It's been quite a while. Since that murder in Massachusetts, I believe. What can I help you with?"

"Well, I know you're taking patients right now, and I was recommended to you by Dr. Vale."

"For yourself?"

"No, not for me. For a very...interesting patient."

"Oh? And who might they be?"

"Do you remember the Northeast Nightmare in Vermont?"

"Why, yes, I heard all about it."

"It's the girl who killed him."

"And what is her name?" the doctor asked curiously.

"Cosette Bordeaux."

"Will this be the first time she will be seeing a psychologist?"

"No, she has been to Dr. Vale before, though that is the only psychotherapy I know her to have had."

"I see. Is that everything you know of her?"

"That's all we know now, although Dr. Vale said she would send her papers if you agreed to take her on," Abberline answered.

"Splendid. Well, I will arrange a session for her then."

Chapter Five:

Cosette glared out the passenger window of the car. Dr. Carnifex's office was not that far away, though Agent Abberline had insisted upon escorting her. The doctor's office was in a neat little two-story building with a gray shingled roof and English ivy growing up the white walls, curling around to the front where there was shrubbery and wooden boxes of fall flowers growing. It didn't look like any psychiatric office she had ever been to; rather it looked pleasant, though this was just the outside, and it said nothing for the people who worked there.

"Well, go inside. You wouldn't want to be late would you?" Abberline said.

"Oh, believe me, I would," Cosette answered sourly, opening the passenger door and getting out.

She shut the car door a little harder than necessary and walked into the building. There was a middle-aged woman with big blonde hair and sparkling, red, cat-eyes glass, and long matching nails sitting behind the front desk. She was talking on the phone, rescheduling an appointment with a patient from the sound of it.

Cosette stood at the front desk, waiting for the woman to finish talking on the phone while examining the things she had behind her desk. There was a large computer, filing cabinets, many pictures of her children, one of whom was graduating, and little candy dishes of sweets for the patients. At last, the woman put the phone away and looked up at her.

"Well, hey there, sweetheart," the woman said in a kindly Texan accent. "Are you here for an appointment?"

"Er, yes, the three o' clock with Dr. Carnifex," Cosette answered.

"Alright, he's running a bit over with his current patient, but he'll be with you briefly. Why don't you have a seat, dear?"

Cosette sat in the armchair nearest the door and examined the lobby. The lobby was a calm, grayish blue with Victorian style paneling. There were many paintings on the walls as well, clearly inspired by the Victorian and Renaissance eras, and all signed "O. C", which Cosette determined meant that the doctor had painted them himself.

There was also a fish tank full of exotic fish, swimming lazily in their decorated containment, a coffee machine sat against one wall; there were books and magazines sitting around to preoccupy the waiting patients, and soft classical music playing from somewhere behind the front desk.

Cosette was just falling into a stupor while staring at the shimmering fish swimming in their tank when there was the sound of a door opening on the second landing and a young man appeared on the stairs escorted by a middle aged man who could only be the doctor. The younger man was crying profusely into a tissue as the doctor spoke comfortingly to him.

"Judith will set up your appointment next week, alright, Gustav? You simply tell her a good time," the doctor was saying.

"Alright, thank you, Doctor," Gustav sniffed. "See you next week."

"Good afternoon, Gustav."

Gustav began talking to Judith, who offered him another tissue and a peppermint stick, both of which he gratefully took. When Gustav was gone, the doctor approached Cosette, smiling gently, his hands clasped behind his back.

He was rather tall and had neat chestnut hair that grayed slightly around his temples and a mustache with the same graying. His face was kind and pleasant, and his eyes, a warm brown, crinkled when he smiled. He wore a pressed white shirt, a yellow tie, and an elbow patch cardigan and altogether seemed very friendly. His presence was somehow comforting, like a childhood memory.

"Hello, you must be Miss Cosette Bordeaux," he said pleasantly.

"And you're Dr. Osiris Carnifex," Cosette returned.

"That's right," the doctor nodded, extending a hand to her.

Cosette examined his hand for a moment but didn't shake it.

"Not to be rude, but shaking hands can transfer about 3,200 bacteria from 150 different species, so if you don't mind, I'd rather not," the girl stated.

"Oh, of course. Thank you for reminding me." Dr. Carnifex said. "Well, do come in. I know I've kept you waiting."

Dr. Carnifex led her up the stairs and opened the door to his office and let them inside. His office was decorated much like the lobby, though a darker blue. Art hung from the walls as well as psychology degrees, and several butterfly collections, pinned up in frames with their scientific name taped underneath them. There were cases of books, interesting trinkets and statues as well as bookshelves built into the walls, lined with many, many books.

"You may sit," Dr. Carnifex remarked to her as he seated himself and adjusted his blazer.

She sat uncertainly in the chair adjacent to the doctor, who had taken up a brown, leather-bound notebook from the side table. Cosette wondered who was supposed to start the conversation as her eyes wandered to the butterflies, pinned behind the glass.

"They're beautiful, aren't they?" Dr. Carnifex remarked, following her eyes.

"It's cruel," Cosette replied.

"Pardon?" the doctor asked.

"They're pinned up in a frame, on display for everyone to

see. It is beauty destroyed by human greed."

Dr. Carnifex looked at her sideways but didn't say anything.

"You don't like eye contact, do you?" he asked at last.

"No," Cosette replied. "It makes me uncomfortable. Eyes say what the mouth can't, or never speak at all. I can tell too much from them or not enough. 'Ah-ha, they're lying!' or 'Are they judging me?'"

"I see. And do you know why Arnold wants you to take counseling with me?"

"Yes. I have to be 'stable' to work with them. Whatever. I don't need counseling. It doesn't work."

"And why do you think that?" Dr. Carnifex asked, crossing his legs and folding his hands.

"Because I've had five already."

"That's quite a lot. Why so many?"

Cosette chuckled darkly to herself.

"Well, I wasn't exactly the most *normal* seven year old. I excelled in school, but my 'people skills' were 'rusty'. So, my parents sent me to a local psychologist who worked with children as well as adults, Dr. Adlea Vale, perhaps you have heard of her?"

"We are acquainted," Dr. Carnifex nodded.

"Yes, well, she diagnosed me with Obsessive Compulsive Disorder, Autism and anxiety—though I would call all of those labels to suffice the understanding of the close-minded," Cosette remarked. "When my parents died, I moved in with my aunt and uncle. Dr. Vale would have been more than willing to do video calls, I'm sure, so movement was hardly the issue. On the contrary, they felt that it would be a blemish on their reputation should anyone find out their orphan niece was *mad*. They would later regret their actions and attempt to find me a proper psychologist—of course, one that fit their standards and beliefs."

"Which would be?" the doctor inquired.

"What they consider normality and the supposed insanity of myself," the girl replied.

"Do you believe yourself to be insane, Cosette?"

"Oh, absolutely. But being mad isn't all that bad," Cosette answered, smiling grimly. "But, back on the latter subject, I was thus tormented by multiple psychologists, but I either ran them off, or they ran my aunt and uncle off until my aunt and uncle decided that I was too much of an embarrassment to go out."

"Do you mean to say they locked you away?"

"They wouldn't call it so. Oh, yes, I could go to and from school. I could grab something from the store if they needed it, but it was simply there and back again and never anywhere else. Not to parties, not to vacations, not to see friends or family—or rather, *their* friends and family. Little did they know, I was glad to be left behind. I didn't want to be around them."

"Would you consider them neglectful?" Dr. Carnifex asked, tapping his pencil rhythmically on his notebook.

"Why, that's quite a judgment call for someone who knows so little of them. Of course, if the judgment is correct, I have no opposition to it being made," Cosette said, standing and straightening her shirt. "But, I know just what you're trying to do. You want me to talk about my *feelings. Boo-hoo.* Well, I know all the tricks in the book, and I doubt you'll be able to crack my casing."

"Of course not," Dr. Carnifex agreed solemnly. "Although, continuing on the topic of your relatives, Arnold said you ran away from home."

"I certainly did," Cosette said, stepping across the room to examine the trinkets on one bookshelf.

"And I suppose your reasoning was because of the way they treated you so horribly?"

"You could say."

"Arnold said he spoke with your aunt and uncle during your investigation."

"What? Why would he talk to them?" Cosette asked, spinning around.

"He was attempting to contact a parent or guardian for your own well-being, but I suppose that didn't go to his plan."

"He didn't tell them where I was, did he?"

"I don't know."

"Well, they wouldn't come looking for me anyways," Cosette sighed, rubbing her eyes.

"How long have you been living alone?" the doctor asked.

"A year," the girl replied. "I was homeless for a while, six months, I believe, but then I started writing mysteries for the paper and soon published some things and earned enough to rent an apartment."

"Ah, yes, I read some of your work. It is exceptional really. And your heroine, Helenor Gray, that would be you?"

"How did you know?" Cosette asked.

"You are very much the same. Besides, in your novel, *Scarlet Reckoning,* Miss Gray also killed the antagonist who attacked her."

Cosette looked suddenly as if she felt sick.

"Do you use writing as an escape?"

Cosette said nothing.

"You are the girl who killed the Northeast Nightmare?"

Cosette didn't reply, but the doctor saw her hands curl into balls, nails digging into her palms.

"Is that why your aunt and uncle made you leave?"

Cosette looked around at him.

"How did you know that?"

"Arnold figured it out. You know, you never deserved that."

"I didn't expect anything more," the girl grumbled. "It was my own fault for going after him."

"You shouldn't blame yourself for the death of the Nightmare," the doctor stated. "Or for what happened to you."

"Why not? Last time I checked, I was the one who went after him while playing at Sherlock. And I was the one who stabbed him," Cosette replied frankly.

"It was in self-defense," Dr. Carnifex said.

Cosette looked away saying nothing.

"Something is on your mind; you can tell it to me," the doctor assured her.

"Tell me, Doctor, where do we draw the line between self-defense and murder?"

"Did you have the intention of murdering him when you first saw him?" the doctor asked.

"No."

"What about after he spoke to you?"

"I wanted to get as far away from him as I could," Cosette said softly.

"I can already tell you it wasn't murder, my dear," the doctor remarked.

"I stabbed him repeatedly. I killed him," Cosette remarked. "And they called me a hero."

"And how does that make you feel knowing that?" Dr. Carnifex asked.

"I see. Well done," the girl remarked suddenly, spinning around to face him. "You've been trying to get me to open up. Well, too bad. I don't want to talk to you anymore."

Dr. Carnifex watched calmly as she turned on her heel and marched towards the door, snapping it shut behind her.

She had not calmed down when she reached the car and slammed the passenger door shut after her.

"What's the matter?" Agent Abberline asked in surprise.

"I don't *want* counseling! I don't *need* counseling! I'm not going back!" the girl remarked.

"You have to," Abberline said.

"Why is that then?"

"I need to know you're able to maintain your stability while working with us."

"Is that because you're so afraid I'll become like those killers? '*She killed once, she could kill again*!'? Don't think I didn't know what you were thinking. Well, you know what? If that's what you think, you can just get up off your lazy ass and solve the crimes like the director you're supposed to be, rather than having a sixteen-year-old do what your whole bloody unit can't seem to manage!"

With that, Cosette let herself out of Abberline's car, leaving a startled Abberline alone and walked herself home.

Chapter Six:

Agent Abberline sighed as he inspected the corpse of a young woman sitting, propped up in one of the floral iron wrought chairs at the table set outside the flower shop. She looked to be in her late twenties with blonde hair and blue eyes. Murdered just like the last woman and missing her ring finger.

Chief Abberline was overseeing the investigation yet again and watching the forensics team, who were already roving about the crime scene, testing for DNA, prints, and fibers. Det. Creed stood beside the print specialist, Edgar Mortensen, who was taking photographs for evidence.

"The Ripper again?" Agent Abberline asked Det. Creed.

"Same as the others. She was killed in an alley, throat slit, missing ring finger, she even resembles the other victims," the head-detective answered, nodding at the corpse.

"Who called in?"

"The florist found her dead when he came in this morning. Apparently she worked here, so leaving her at a flower shop wasn't just a show of his demented romanticism, he knew someone would find her here within a few hours of the murder."

Just then a red BMW pulled up to the crime scene and Dr. Vale stepped out. She fetched her red handbag out of the passenger seat and went to greet Agent Abberline, Det.Creed, and the chief.

"Hi, Arnold. Carol, it's so good to see you again!" Dr. Vale said, giving the chief a quick hug.

"I'm so glad Arnold managed to contact you. He said he sent you with copies of the files on the Ripper's case. Were you able to go over them yet?" Chief Abberline asked her.

"Yes, I did. Arnold called me again a while ago when he got news of the crime scene. He wanted me to come down and see if I noticed anything," Dr. Vale said.

"Well, have you found anything so far? About the conversations they had over the phone, I mean?" Agent Abberline asked.

"Well, I noticed that the Ripper seems like a very amiable person—at least over the phone. In fact, it's very clear that he's *trying* to be friendly and kind. It's as if he was copying what he had seen in romance movies. I'm not certain he has a very high social intellect. One thing I do know is that he wanted Miss Alfreds to like him. He was doing everything he could to gain her trust and affection. I know I've diagnosed him with sociopathy, but there's something off about his luring methods," Dr. Vale remarked.

"Why would he want these women to like him?" Det. Creed asked. "Especially if he's just going to slaughter them?"

"Perhaps he doesn't have a clear sense of right and wrong. I mean, look at the way he leaves his victims, he respects them at least somewhat."

Surprised at the new voice, they turned around to see Cosette standing there, inspecting the crime scene with her hands behind her back.

"What are you doing here?" Agent Abberline asked, surprised to see her.

"News travels fast, especially to me," Cosette replied. "Have you checked her phone?"

"We have it, but we haven't looked at it yet," Chief Abberline said.

"I would recommend doing that," the girl said.

"What do you mean he 'respects' them?" Det. Creed asked

her.

"I mean that he kills them so that they'll die within a few minutes and then leaves them where they can be found quickly."

"Or he just wants to show off his work," Creed said.

"Or that. But I noticed that he kills a specific looking type of woman," Cosette mused. "Which would mean that they remind him of something or someone. Maybe a traumatic situation, or something that drove him to insanity."

"So either this is respect or revenge," the chief said.

"Hello, Cosette, do you remember me?"

Cosette looked around, her eyes falling on Dr. Vale and inspected her.

"Yes, I remember you, Dr. Vale. Are you assisting on this case again?"

"Yes, I'm the behavioral analyst," Dr. Vale nodded with a smile.

"The woman apparently fought back. We need to get the body back to the morgue for testing. We may be able to extract some DNA," Allan Mortensen remarked, coming over.

"Alright, go ahead," the chief replied.

"Can I ask to see the files of the current victims?" Cosette asked.

"It's against the rules to let civilians see our private records," Det. Creed began.

"I make the rules, Det. Creed," Chief Abberline said. "And I know that it is perfectly fine for her to see them. Dr. Vale, you should come along as well."

Creed glared at Cosette, who grinned back at him, rocking on her heels.

"Oh, Abberline! Agent Abberline!"

Agent Abberline sighed as he turned around to face Pandora Crestmont and Conrad Finnigan, Pandora waving her recorder in the air above her. He knew she would be back sooner or later; he just wished it was later.

"Agent Abberline, could you comment on the latest murder? Who is she? You know for a fact it's the Richmond Ripper now, don't you? Do you think you'll finally catch him or fail miserably like last time?" Pandora asked, the words falling from her mouth and into the recorder in a torrent.

"No comments," Agent Abberline replied.

Pandora sighed as if she had expected the answer and turned to Det. Creed.

"Det. Creed, could you elaborate on the—"

"No. And no one else here will, so just go home, Ms. Crestmont," Det. Creed cut her off, shoving the recorder out of his face.

Pandora growled, stomping her heeled foot, and turned to click back to her car, barking for Conrad to follow.

"I'm sure there's something we can put her in a jail cell for, I've just got to figure out what," the chief sighed.

Cosette went to stand by the chief's car, waiting to be driven to the station to continue their investigation. It wasn't long before Dr. Vale came for her car, which was beside Chief Abberline's.

"I heard you started counseling with Dr. Carnifex," Dr. Vale said upon seeing the girl.

"Yes, I've been to a singular session," Cosette replied.

"And how was it? Did you enjoy it?"

"Not particularly," the girl admitted.

"Oh, well, when I recommended Dr. Carnifex, I thought that you would connect well with him."

"Oh, *you're* the one who recommended him to Abberline," Cosette grumbled.

"You don't sound pleased at all," Dr. Vale said worriedly.

"Fascinating deduction, Dr, Vale," Cosette replied. "Congratulations on a correct one."

Dr. Vale realized that talking to Cosette wasn't doing anything but agitating her, so they stayed silent while they waited beside the cars for the chief.

Cosette wandered a little ways from the chief's car and wondered about the murders, kicking a rock along the sidewalk, thinking, when Pandora Crestmont appeared at her shoulder.

"Hi, sweetie. I saw that you were talking to Agent Abberline and the rest of the department. What were they telling you about?" Pandora asked, bending down to Cosette's level.

"They weren't telling me anything," Cosette replied tersely.

"Then why were you across the caution tape?"

Cosette shrugged.

"Were you supposed to be there?"

"Yeah."

"Why? Are you helping them in some way? Aren't you a little young for that?"

"I don't know, aren't you a little too young to be a sleazy, cheating reporter who sold her soul to a newspaper just for the thrill and the attention?" Cosette replied dryly, causing Pandora to look at her in surprise and indignation. "Oh, yes, I know who you are. I sell my work to the paper rivaling yours, *The Virginia Times*."

"But you're only—what—fourteen?"

"Sixteen, actually," the girl corrected.

"And what's your name, *sweetie*?" Pandora asked with evident venom.

"Cosette H. Bordeaux—the 'H' is for Helenor."

Pandora raised her eyebrows and stepped back a moment to size the girl up. She then put a hand on her hip.

"*You're* Cosette Bordeaux?" she drawled disbelievingly, crossing her arms over her chest.

"That's what my birth certificate says."

"You write those mystery stories published in the Times? What was that one everyone was talking about? *Scarlet Reckoning*?"

"Yes, the hardback is coming out soon if you'd like a copy."

"Actually, I didn't think it was that good," Pandora remarked, turning up her nose.

"Well, not everyone has taste," Cosette replied nonchalantly.

"Humph! What would the FBI and the VPD want with you

anyway?"

"Much like you, I'm putting my nose where it doesn't belong for the sake of a story. There are only two differences between us. Do you want to know what they are?"

Pandora raised an eyebrow in question.

"Well, go on then," she said irritatedly.

"First, I actually have the rights to the story. Second, my work isn't flaming trash."

Pandora turned as red as her dress and clenched her gloved fists. Cosette watched in interest, wondering if the woman might burst a vein.

"Hey, what's going on here?" Chief Abberline asked, coming up behind them. "Cosette, come away from her. Let's go. We're meeting the others at the station."

Cosette curtsied to Pandora before running to get inside the chief's car, leaving Pandora looking furious.

"Do *not* talk to Pandora Crestmont," Chief Abberline said as soon as they drove away. "She's trouble."

"Oh, I know. She works with *The Richmond Exposée*, which is worse than any tabloid. I know her reputation well—or rather those she's ruined. I wouldn't even tell her the weather."

"Then what were you two talking about?"

"Oh, *Scarlet Reckoning* is getting a hardback. I simply told her so."

"You know, Arnold told me about what happened with Dr. Carnifex. He didn't think you were coming back."

"I wasn't going to, but I can't give up a story like this to someone like Pandora."

When they all arrived at the station, the chief went to her office where her husband, Det. Creed and Dr. Vale were waiting.

"Det. Knox, I want all the files on the Richmond Ripper's victims," she called to the junior detective as they walked through.

"Yes, ma'am, I'll grab them right away," Seymour said, hurrying to the file room.

When Seymour returned with the files, he promptly

tripped over his own two feet, spilling the papers onto the floor, and then had to regain himself and pick it all up, before hurrying away embarrassedly.

Cosette took a look at the files for a moment. They were all women of similar appearance and age, some single, some in relationships or married, but there was nothing different about any of their deaths.

"Are you certain these are *all* the victims of the Ripper?" Cosette asked finally.

"As far as we know," Chief Abberline answered. "Well, I say that."

"What do you mean?"

"There was a similar case a couple years ago, but it wasn't the Richmond Ripper. It was some other man. Killed his wife only a year after their marriage. But there is no connection to the Ripper. Det. Creed closed that case and the man was locked up."

"I wouldn't be so sure about all that. Let me see the man's file."

The file was fetched—this time without Seymour botching it—and Cosette took a look at it.

"It says here that he stabbed her thrice and then slit her throat and cut off her finger, just as the Ripper's victims. When the police arrived, the killer, Thomas Herrod is his name, was found stabbed as well, though he survived and was incarcerated. Why was he stabbed?"

"Of his own actions. To evade the law, he admitted it in court," Det. Creed replied.

"Why would he kill his wife and then try to commit suicide?" Cosette asked. "That's senseless."

"Well, he was guilty of uxoricide," Dr. Vale remarked. "Murder alone can make people turn to suicide in an attempt to evade punishment, guilt, and even scorn, but murder of wife or family can make it a hundred times worse."

"Besides, Herrod already admitted to his crime. Det. Creed was the one who found proof of the evidence against him, and he's our best detective," the chief remarked, and Creed swelled with silent pride.

"But it doesn't make sense. I want to talk to Mr. Herrod, if you wouldn't mind."

"Why? You think I can't do my job?" Det. Creed snapped at her.

"That isn't what I said. But part of *your job* is checking all the angles. Perhaps you should do that then," the girl said.

Chapter Seven:

Chief Abberline had scheduled an appointment for Cosette to meet Thomas Herrod, the supposed murderer. In the meantime, Cosette returned home in order for the police to make such arrangements.

"This is ridiculous," Det. Creed groaned when she had gone. "Why are we letting a ten-year-old run around solving murders like she's been sporting a badge for eighteen years?"

"Because she can notice the little things and that's what counts," Agent Creed answered. "We don't need her often, but when and if we do, she tells us something like 'Why would Herrod try to kill himself instead of running?'"

"Anybody could have noticed that," Creed grumbled.

"You didn't when you were investigating him," Dr. Vale pointed out.

Det. Creed glared at her and turned to go off to his own desk, but the chief stopped him.

"Look," she sighed, pulling him aside. "I've avoided talking about this, but seeing as how she's arriving this afternoon, and you're already in a bad enough mood, I ought to prepare you."

"What are you talking about? Who's arriving?" Det. Creed asked, eying her in confusion.

"Your new partner."

"What? No. I don't need a partner, I've told you that!"

Creed exclaimed angrily.

"I know you don't want a partner after Emrys, but you've been a stand-alone detective for almost a year, and everyone else has a partner."

"I'm not everyone else; I'm the head-detective," Creed insisted. "And I've been working fine alone."

"Tell me, Alastor, how many times have you had to reload your gun on cases?" Chief Abberline asked.

Det. Creed's face darkened, and he crossed his arms.

"Enough times to get the job done," he grumbled. "I don't know why that matters."

"Because you have shot more criminals than ever I have seen a detective shoot in the last year," the chief replied, raising her eyebrow at him.

"But did they die?" Creed returned.

"Some."

"They attacked or had hostages."

"You need someone to cool you off when you get trigger-happy," the chief remarked. "You are my best detective and I can't lose you. That's final."

Det. Creed was terribly irritated the rest of the day. He worked on the Ripper case some more and went over all the files on Thomas Herrod and his murder claim as well as the videos that had been taken during the court trials to see if there was anything he had missed while investigating him. He was so enthralled in his work that he had nearly forgotten completely about the arrival of his new partner.

That afternoon, a woman entered the police station, and, in her hands, she carried a large cardboard box. She was beautiful with long, wavy, sunkissed hair, sparkling ocean eyes and a bright smile that showed all her perfect, white teeth. She was talking to Lesly at the front desk, and a minute later, she nodded in understanding of something and headed for the chief's office. She knocked and went inside.

Det. Creed had only taken brief notice of her before returning to his work. Chief Abberline exited her office followed by the woman a while later, and they made their way to Det. Creed's desk.

"Um...hello?" the head-detective said questioningly. "Who are you?"

"Det. Creed, this is your new partner," the chief introduced.

"Hi, I'm Det. Eleanor Everglow," the woman said cheerfully, extending her hand. "It's so exciting to be in Virginia. California is so different, you know. *Way* sunnier."

Det. Creed didn't shake her hand nor did he return any form of introduction whatsoever, but only glared blankly at her.

"So, how long have you been a detective?" Det. Creed asked at last.

"Ten years," Det. Everglow answered. "I'm originally from Kansas, but I worked in Los Angeles, and then I was transferred over here. It's definitely more promising, since I'm suddenly a head-detective's partner. I didn't even have a partner in L. A."

"I've had partners before, but I prefer working alone," Det. Creed remarked bluntly. "Too bad it couldn't stay that way."

"Oh, well, I'm sure we'll make a great team," Det. Everglow replied surely, setting her box down on the desk.

"What is that?" Creed asked.

"Oh, it's my stuff," Everglow answered.

"You mean we're supposed to share a desk?" he asked the chief.

"You *are* partners after all. So you should treat her with such respect," Chief Abberline said overtly.

"Yeah, yeah, whatever. If you'll excuse me, I've got to talk to Mortensen about Herrod's 'attempted suicide'. He may be able to tell whether or not it really was that.

"Oh, you're already working on a case?" Det. Everglow asked.

"I am, you're not. I already have enough tagalongs on this one," Creed replied bluntly.

"Don't worry, I'll give you the case file later," the chief told Everglow privately.

Det. Creed grumbled to himself about this as he took the files to show the chief coroner and went out to his car.

He arrived at the morgue in five minutes and went inside to Mortensen's office. Ebenizer Mortensen was a rather strange little man, but Det. Creed supposed you had to be strange in at least some sense to cut people open and examine their insides. He was about sixty years old, with wispy silver and white hair, and white eyes. His skin was as pale and blotchy in places, and he could easily have been mistaken for one of the corpses he inspected.

"Ah, Det. Creed, what brings you here today?" Mortensen asked, clapping his hands together, clasping them behind his back and rocking on his heels.

"Take a look at these pictures," Creed said, tossing the Manilla folder on the mortuary table.

Mortensen opened the folder and examined the photographs inside.

"What are these?"

"The wounds from Thomas Herrod's suicide attempt. You weren't on the case, but I'm sure you heard about it."

"I did, yes."

"I want you to tell me whether or not this was an actual suicide attempt or if these were inflicted by an attacker," Creed said, tapping the photograph.

"That's very hard to tell from a photograph alone," Mortensen replied unsurely.

"Well, it's all we've got to go off of, and you're going to have to figure something out seeing as how this could be vital to the Richmond Ripper case."

"Well, it might take a little bit of time, but I'll see what I can do," Mortensen said. "It's been a while since I've had a challenge anyways. By the way, are you on your lunch break any time soon?"

"In five minutes," Creed answered, checking his watch. "Why?"

"Do you think you could grab me some peanut butter

while I look at these? I ran out—gotta have something to go with these pickles!" Mortensen chuckled, pulling a jar of pickles out of the morgue freezer.

Creed raised his eyebrows but agreed to do this, thinking he ought to grab a bite to eat himself.

He felt like getting a burger, so he went out to a local mom-and-pop place that he favored. He ate in thinking that it wasn't too favorable to eat around dead bodies. When he had finished up, he stopped by the grocery store and grabbed a jar of peanut butter for Mortensen and went back to the morgue.

"Ah, Det. Creed, so glad you're back. And you brought peanut butter. Thank you ever so kindly."

Creed then watched impatiently as Mortensen made himself a peanut butter and pickle sandwich with one of his spare surgical knives.

"Are you done?" Creed asked when the sandwich was made.

"Yes. And, I also made progress on the photos you brought me," Mortensen remarked.

"What did you find?" Creed asked.

Mortensen retrieved the pictures and laid them out on the mortuary table.

"Well, it's a long shot seeing as how the wounds are all in places easily accessed, but what I noticed was that they aren't on point. It looks as though whoever had the knife was stabbing while Herrod was struggling. Besides, look at these cuts and bruises. They look like defense wounds."

"I knew it. I told Abberline we should've brought all this to you the first time around."

"I'm not sure why you didn't," Mortensen agreed.

"Maybe it's because you make peanut butter and pickle sandwiches with the same surgical knife you use to conduct autopsies?" Creed suggested.

"But everybody does that!" Mortensen replied.

"No, no one does that, Ebenezer."

"Well, anyway, the stab wounds could be mistaken for

someone hesitantly and blindly stabbing out in desperation for the end. It's obvious though that these cuts and bruises are from self-defense. I'll continue over these pictures and see if I can find anything else to prove this as a definite attack."

❀❀❀

Creed returned to the station after leaving the morgue. As soon as he walked in, he saw that Det. Everglow was sitting at his desk. Deciding that he didn't want to talk to her, he went around the station, entering through the back door and going to Chief Abberline's office.

"Dective, you're back," the chief said. "What did Mortensen say?"

"He said that although the stab wounds are in locations that would be easily accessed during an attempt, a self-inflicted wound would be more hesitant and therefore less severe—of course, the location of the wounds could be mistaken for that, but it seemed as though Herrod had been struggling, and these were far more intense, as well as the fact that there were multiple of these intense wounds, which seems slightly implausible. We also dug up notices of cuts and bruises that had been on his body afterwards. They were assumed to be from his wife in her attempted escape, but Mortensen said that they seemed more like his own self-defense."

"Which could ultimately mean that he was attacked by the same person who killed his wife."

"Which means the Ripper tried to kill both of them."

"But why?" the chief pondered. "He only goes after women."

Just then the door opened, and Everglow entered.

"Oh, hi, Alastor, you're back! I didn't see you come in. I hope I'm not interrupting anything, I just had to file some stuff about my arrival," she said.

"Yeah, that's great, anyway, as I was saying, they were the only married couple out of all the victims. Maybe that had something to do with it," Creed suggested.

"Are you talking about Amanda Herrod's murder? It really

was the Ripper, wasn't it? Maybe he meant to only kill the woman, but the man witnessed it," Everglow suggested.

"That's a good point," the chief said. "You haven't been here an hour, and you're already solving cases."

"Well, give her the key to the city. She's doing her job," Det. Creed muttered.

"So it seems that Mr. Herrod might have been lying to us all along," Chief Abberline said. "And I want to know why he would take the fall for a killer if he did nothing wrong, which means we'll definitely need to talk to him."

Chapter Eight:

Mr. Thomas Herrod was an average looking man, with tan skin, short brown hair, and brown eyes. He was of average height and weight, with hardly anything interesting about him except his limp and the stubble he had gained from his time behind bars. Cosette, though, looked at him as if he were a very interesting painting.

No one had spoken for at least ten minutes since their arrival. Det. Creed huffed a few times in the girl's direction, but she didn't seem to recognize the existence of anyone but herself and the prisoner. At last, Cosette sighed and shifted her weight to her other leg, placing a hand on her hip.

"You didn't kill Amanda Herrod," she accused.

"What makes you think that?" Herrod chuckled.

"You haven't got blood on your hands," the girl replied.

"Well, of course I washed it off years ago," the man replied with an amused smile.

"I *mean* that I know what a killer looks like, and you aren't it."

"You're just a little girl. How can you tell if I killed someone or not?" Herrod asked.

"Do your hands always shake like that?" Cosette asked, inspecting the man's trembling hands, which he held down by his sides to make them less conspicuous.

Herrod stuffed his hands in his pockets.

"You haven't guilt—though not all killers are remorseful. But you...you're afraid of something, Mr. Herrod. What are you afraid of? You're already in jail, so it can't be that you're afraid of the law. If I didn't know any better I'd say you feel safer in jail. Why would you say that is?"

"Well, think of it—no bills, free food, all I have to do is sit around all day besides a little exercise, suffering through happy group counseling hour and whatnot. I've even taken some meds for my depression. It ain't half bad."

"That's a truly horrible pretext. Let me repeat myself. You did not kill Amanda Herrod," Cosette stated.

"I killed Amanda Herrod," Herrod remarked with a grin.

"How?"

"I slit her throat and cut off her ring finger," the convict replied. "Then I tried to kill myself. Too bad it didn't work."

"Why would you want to kill her? It seemed you had a pretty good relationship according to your file."

"Well, I don't know what you heard, but we fought all the time. I couldn't stand her honestly. Then one day, I just got fed up, I guess."

"That's funny, because you killed her in the exact same manner the Richmond Ripper kills his victims," Cosette said.

Herrod looked at her strangely for a moment, as if something in him had been triggered by the title.

"I guess that's just coincidence," he shrugged finally. "Or perhaps I have an admirer."

"There's no such thing as coincidence, Mr. Herrod," Cosette said. "Now, tell me, why would you want to commit suicide?"

"I was obviously shocked at the realization of what I had done. I didn't want to go to jail; I just didn't want to have to pay for a divorce. It was the only thing I could think of to do to get out of the situation I was about to find myself in."

"That's funny, because our coroner inspected the old pictures of your wounds, and he said it sure looks like you have a lot of defense wounds," Det. Creed spoke up.

"My wife—"

"Don't say 'My wife fought back'. We know it's bullshit," Creed stopped him irritatedly.

Herrod frowned.

"Who really killed your wife, Mr. Herrod?" the chief asked.

"I did," Herrod said.

"But why? Simply in a moment of anger?" Cosette asked, cocking her head to one side.

"Wrath is the worst of the sins," Herrod answered.

"That's a stupid reason to kill someone then," the girl remarked.

This comment caused both Agent Abberline and Det. Creed to have to hold their laughter.

"You're awfully rude, aren't you?" Herrod said, though he was clearly amused by her.

"I'm not rude; I'm honest. No one would read a story about a murder like that. It's too cliché," Cosette replied.

"Maybe I'm just cliché then."

Cosette sighed and then turned away from Herrod to Chief Abberline.

"I'd like to see Mrs. Herrod's file once more, but otherwise, I need nothing more from him at the moment," she said.

"Alright, I think you covered all our questions as well. Let's go back and see what else we can dig up. The judge should have sent me all Herrod's court files for you to look over," the chief said.

As they were leaving, though, Herrod beckoned to Cosette before she could leave.

"You won't be able to prove I didn't kill my wife," Herrod told her. "Not that I didn't. I did."

"Is that a challenge?"

"If you want it to be," Herrod replied.

Cosette gave a half-smile and turned to leave, but was called back again.

"Hey!"

"Yes?" she inquired, turning around once more.

"Do you know what makes a crane like a red herring?" Herrod asked her.

"I'm not entirely sure, Mr. Herrod. What makes a crane like a red herring?" the girl asked.

"Figure it out yourself, little Miss Detective," the man replied with a devilish grin and waggled his finger at her.

She rolled her eyes and exited the jail to find the Abberlines, Creed, and Dr. Vale waiting outside for her.

"What did he want?" the director asked.

"He said I wouldn't be able to prove he didn't kill his wife," Cosette related. "And then he asked me 'What makes a crane like a red herring?'."

"Well, what was the answer?" Det. Creed asked.

"He said that I'd have to figure that out on my own."

"That's stupid," Creed remarked.

"Though perhaps it's a clue. Whatever he meant by that riddle could be an important clue in this case" Chief Abberline said.

"Well, he's either sociopathic, or he didn't kill his wife," Dr. Vale remarked. "Cosette's right; he didn't show any signs of remorse when he spoke about killing his wife. It was like some sort of act he was putting on. I agree with what Cosette has said."

"Let's go back to the station and see what we can come up with," the chief suggested.

Cosette got in the chief's car, and Dr. Vale took her car, while Creed returned with the director.

"What she just did back there—that 'detective work'--was something I could have done with my eyes closed," Det. Creed remarked as they drove.

"Then why don't you?" Agent Abberline returned.

"Because you only want to hear what *Cosette* finds. She doesn't even have a badge. With all due respect, sir, you are giving me none. You shouldn't have some kid you found on the street working a case with us."

"Okay, why don't you tell her that she's not on the case

anymore, because the last time I checked, she said she quit, came back a few days later, found a mistake *you* had made with a victim who was most likely actually killed by the Ripper and will figure out how to force her way back into the case if I let her go," Agent Abberline said.

"Why does she want to help us so badly anyway? We don't need her help," Creed grumbled.

"I told her she could publish this case as a fictional novel if she helped us a bit."

"What! Why would you do that?"

Abberline shrugged.

"It was the only reason she'd help besides money. In fact, I'd say it's more about the story, less about the money."

"Well, now we'll never get rid of her. She won't stop until she has an end for her book," Creed grumbled.

❀❀❀

In the chief's car, Cosette frowned as she looked through the file in her hands.

"Something's wrong," Cosette said.

They had gone to the station and grabbed the files on the victims so Cosette could examine them.

"Well, no shit, Sherlock," Det. Creed remarked, pacing the room back and forth.

"Hush, Alastor," Chief Abberline said.

"Did you ever take into consideration that the Ripper has killed a lot of women on the same day in different years?"

"Yes, but it wasn't repetitive enough for us to add it to the Ripper's pattern," Creed replied.

"What relevance does this particular day have to The Richmond Ripper?" Cosette asked.

"We don't know," Chief Abberline said. "We didn't have enough evidence to connect it to anything."

"I think the killer was married," Cosette said. "Or at least he *was* married."

"You think he killed his wife?" Agent Abberline asked.

"That's actually completely possible. Serial killers have

been known to kill on days that are relevant to them," Dr. Vale agreed.

"So is it possible that the day he had most repeatedly killed these people is some sort of anniversary relevant to him and/or his wife?"

"It's very much possible," the chief answered.

"If we can connect the anniversary to a person, we could possibly nail the Ripper," Det. Creed said.

"I would recommend you start off looking for marriage anniversaries and obituary dates on the same day," Cosette said. "Make sure they're married and check out the husbands; one of them is probably the Ripper."

Chapter Nine:

Cosette had arrived at Dr. Carnifex's office early, and Judith had told her that she could wait outside the doctor's door until he finished his session. Soon enough, he opened the door and saw his patient, Gustav, out before showing Cosette inside.

"Hello, Cosette. I haven't kept you waiting too long, have I?" Dr. Carnifex asked, taking up his notebook from his desk.

"Not at all," Cosette replied.

"Then I won't keep you waiting any longer. Come, have a seat," the doctor said, sitting down himself. "You know, I didn't think you would return after our last session."

"I didn't either," Cosette replied. "But I have some questions—and, of course, it's mandatory to be here if I want to work with the FBI on this case."

"What would you like to discuss this session then? Perhaps we should pick up where we left off?" the doctor suggested.

"I'd rather not frankly."

"I see," Dr. Carnifex hummed, crossing one leg over the other.

They sat in silence, Cosette examining the red nail polish chipping off her fingers while the doctor inspected her for any signs of emotion.

"But tell me, Doctor," Cosette said suddenly, as if they had been conversing for hours. "Could someone be so horrified by their past actions that they find themselves forced to repeat those same actions over again?"

"Why, yes, it's not that uncommon, especially with trauma."

"Could that apply to murder?"

"Yes. In fact, some people speculate that Jack the Ripper killed because he was disgusted by his own lust. Why?"

"I believe that is why the Richmond Ripper kills. He's so distraught and horrified with grief and guilt. He killed his wife, and that is why he kills other women who look like her to ease the guilt," Cosette remarked.

"Do you feel guilt?"

"What?"

"Do you feel guilty for killing Antony Sanguini?"

Cosette contemplated her shoes.

"I don't know what I feel," she answered at last.

"Why would you say that?"

"Because I'm afraid they aren't real. You know, I can feel other people's emotions, but I can never distinguish my own."

"You can *feel* other people's emotions?"

"Yes, I can tell when people lie, when they're angry, sad, or afraid. I know when they hate me or don't want to be around me, sometimes I still make people uncomfortable without knowing it though."

"Do people hate you?" Dr. Carnifex asked.

"Yes."

"How do you know people hate you? Ah, but you said you can 'sense' it. Rather, *why* do you think people hate you?"

"Well, I'd say 'They hate me because I'm different,' but that's quite cliché. So I will say that I am rather rude, whether unintentionally or not; I have a tendency to speak my mind, which frankly perturbs people; any associates find me irritating because I am better at my job than them at only sixteen—and the fact that I am aware of it, of course. They call it arrogance, though I suppose it could come across as such. Besides, I'm mentally ill and committed third degree murder."

"Are you a killer, Cosette?" the doctor asked.

"Yes," she replied.

"Killers want to hurt people. Killers don't care how many people they kill, or who they kill. Killers kill with intent. You killed in self defense. That isn't murder."

Cosette didn't speak, but stood and went across the room to examine one of the glass cases, though Dr. Carnifex could feel her silent disagreement.

"What do you feel, Cosette?" Dr. Carnifex asked after some silence.

"Be more specific. All the time? This morning? Right now? About the weather?"

"What do you feel about killing Saungini?"

"Nothing," Cosette replied, inspecting a small, glass red dragon sitting in one of the doctor's cases.

Dr. Carnifex scratched something onto his notepad.

"What does the Richmond Ripper feel, Cosette?"

"Grief, guilt, sorrow, regret, remorse, hatred. He can't get his own actions out of his head. He can't forget."

"Have you ever hated yourself, Cosette?"

Cosette didn't answer.

"Doctor, do you believe in God?" the girl asked suddenly.

"I was baptized Catholic, though I find I do not believe in God," Dr. Carnifex replied.

"That's stupid," Cosette remarked.

"How so?" the doctor asked.

"Well, I find that every time I try to imagine how the universe was created, I think of the Big Bang Theory. But what brought that about? We don't really know, do we? And so on and so on until we must ultimately bring creation back to some higher power. I like to believe that higher power is God. But God is, of course, something that you cannot see, touch or hear, so then how can we know He exists? Well, how can we know that darkness exists? We can't see it. We can't feel it. We can't hear it. It is the absence of light. But in that absence, our brains recognize it as something, darkness. The same premise can be used for the existence of God," Cosette remarked.

Dr. Carnifex only smiled.

"How very interesting."

"Well, anyways, I'm going to hell."

"Why, what makes you think that?" Dr. Carnifex asked, mildly surprised.

"I'm afraid God can't forgive me."

"There's always confession. Why not try that?"

"Oh, I do," Cosette replied. "But I find I confess the same sins over and over again. I must be rather stupid to repeat the same old mistakes."

"The Richmond Ripper must be rather stupid too then."

"Yes, I suppose so," Cosette agreed.

"I would recommend only going to confession once a month—and that is only if you *require* it. Perhaps consider speaking with a priest about what merits confession. May I ask what you confess?"

"What do you think?" Cosette muttered.

"I think you repeatedly confess the death of the Northeast Nightmare."

"Bingo."

Chapter Ten:

"Okay, Alastor, the chief filled me in on everything going on, gave me the files and stuff, and went ahead and did a run down on all the men who were married on or around this specific day," Everglow reported, setting the papers down on their desk and sitting down herself.

"That's a lot of men to look through," Creed said disinterestedly.

"Well, I only looked through the ones whose wives were deceased, so there weren't too many and only the ones who died suspiciously."

"Uh-huh," Creed said without looking up from his laptop. "So, uh...what did you find anyhow?"

"Well, there are about twenty-four widowed men in Virginia, all of whom had wives that fit the description of the Ripper's victims, though I counted most of them out because they weren't married around the same time as the Ripper kills—or rather his 'Marriage Anniversary'."

"Let me see the file," Det. Creed said, holding out his hand for the Manilla folder.

He sighed out of his nostrils as he flipped through the folder. It only took him a moment to look through all of it before he tossed it back to the young woman.

"Get rid of any men who got married before 2014," Creed

said.

"Alright," Everglow said and removed the specific ones.

Det. Creed took another look at it and nodded.

"So now we just have to figure out which one is our guy."

"Well, D. Washburn's and M. Turner's wives both died in car wrecks," Det. Everglow said. "But they were hit by drunk drivers."

"Do we have records of that?"

"Yes, right here, so they're automatically ruled out."

"Okay, and what else?"

"A. George's wife died of an allergic reaction to a corn dog that was fried in peanut oil."

"Are there medical records of that?"

"Yes, there are records of that too."

"That leaves us with five men."

"Print out their photographs and copy the files for me," Det. Creed ordered.

Det. Everglow went down the hall to the printer and printed out the photos as well as a copy of the file. She tucked them neatly into a Manilla folder and handed them to the head-detective.

"I also added each man's basic personal information just in case you might need to look over it.

"Thanks," Creed said, taking the file from her and standing from their desk.

He tucked the folder under his arm in order to adjust his tie. He took up his coat as he headed for the door, though he didn't stop when Det. Everglow called, "Where are you going?"

"To see Herod. And no, I'm not bringing you along," he replied.

He left the station and got in his car, which was parked out front, and left his partner looking offended on the sidewalk.

When he arrived at the prison, he parked and went directly to Thomas Herrod's cell.

"Herrod," the head-detective greet solemnly.

Thomas Herrod did not stir nor show any signs that he

was aware of the man's presence.

"I've brought a file containing the information on several men who we think may be the Richmond Ripper. We *could* just interrogate them separately, but it would be *so* much easier if you could just identify the killer."

The convict still gave no reply.

"I wouldn't ignore me if I were you."

"What are you going to do if I ignore you, Detective? Arrest me?" Herrod grinned.

"Well, this could very well be your ticket out of here. Oh, but I forgot, you don't *want* to get out. But don't worry, if you want to stay in here so badly, we'll make sure you do. But still, do us all a favor and look at the damn file," Det. Creed growled.

"Haven't I told you already that the Richmond Ripper has nothing to do with dear, dead, Amanda? It's just a coincidence that we killed our victims the same way, you see. But you already know all this, Detective; you are the one who arrested me after all. But, then, you aren't humbling yourself to admit that you might have gotten the wrong man, aren't you?"

"Hardly. I'm simply considering another angle."

Herrod chuckled.

"Still, I won't tell you anything."

"Alastor!"

Det. Creed turned to see Det. Everglow hurrying up to him, waving a few pieces of paper in the air.

"I forgot to put in one of the suspect's information so I figured I'd bring it down myself. But I'm sure you don't mind. That's what partners are for after all, right?" Det. Everglow said with a hint of force.

"Who is *this*?" Herrod drawled.

"Oh, hi, I'm Det. Eleanor Everglow. Nice to meet you."

"My pleasure," Herrod replied smoothly.

"Sweet Jesus," Creed murmured in disgust, rubbing his face. "Will you at least talk to *her* then?"

"She's far nicer than you, and far nicer to look at, certainly," Herrod remarked. "But no."

"Is there anyone you *will* talk to about this bloody case?" Creed exclaimed irritatedly.

"Well…the only person I'll talk to is little Miss Holmes," Herrod answered at last.

"You mean Cosette?" Det. Creed asked.

"Yes, she's very interesting to talk to."

"Fine," Creed sighed. "I'll call the chief."

Chief Abberline picked up the phone and was glad to hear what the detectives had put together so far and said she would see if Cosette was willing to come down.

She called Cosette multiple times, six times exactly, though the girl never picked up. Perhaps she had just forgotten her phone or was ignoring it. Or perhaps she had fallen into some trouble…

No, she would call her one more time before she sent someone over to check on her. She was just calling her a while later when her husband walked into her office.

"Hey, hun. Just wanted to drop by on my lunch break," Agent Abberline remarked, kissing her on the cheek as he sat down. "I brought you your salad and chicken sandwich by the way."

He set their lunches down on the desk.

"Who are you calling?" he asked.

"I was just calling Cosette. Creed and Everglow dug up some potential suspects and went down to the prison to try and get some more information out of Herrod, but he said he would only talk to Cosette," the chief said.

"Is she going down there now?" Agent Abberline asked, between bites.

"No, she wouldn't pick up."

"Do you want me to go down and see if she needs a ride?" the director asked.

"Yes, I'd appreciate that very much."

Agent Abberline decided to take the rest of his lunch with him and drove down to Cosette's apartment.

When he arrived, he rapped on her door until he heard

the lock click and the door creaked open to reveal Cosette, looking annoyed and quite disheveled, her hair sticking out messier than usual, and still in her pajamas.

"I didn't wake you, did I?" Abberline asked, checking his watch to see that it was nearly the afternoon.

"I've been up for approximately eight hours, thirty-eight minutes and—" Here she glanced back at the clock on the wall across the room. "—Forty-two seconds."

"Ah, I see. Well, Creed and Everglow went to interrogate Mr. Herrod at the prison and he says he'll talk to no one but you."

"Oh," Cosette said. "So that's why the chief was calling me all morning?"

"Yes, that is why. Why didn't you pick up?"

"Personal matters," Cosette replied.

"Ah, I see. I hope we didn't bother you terribly."

"No. But, um, the director of the Behavioral Analysis Unit is at my front door because...?"

"Ah, I was on my lunch break and thought I might as well give you a ride."

"I haven't eaten, I haven't showered, I haven't done my hair, and I'm not leaving until I've checked those things off my list."

"Well, can't you just comb your hair, change your clothes and we can get lunch on the way?" the director suggested.

Cosette looked at him as if he had just remarked that the earth was flat.

"My apologies, but I am not a man. I would prefer not to exit my house looking like a pigsty," she remarked grimly.

"Oh," Abberline said, wondering if he should be offended, though he could tell Cosette clearly wouldn't budge until she had done what she needed to do. "I suppose I'll wait for you then."

"Great," Cosette said, shutting the door in his face.

Abberline shook his head muttering about how all girls must make themselves up before they leave the house and how much of a pain that really was. He heard the water running inside the apartment and called Det. Creed to tell him that Cosette *was* coming to the prison but it would take them a while to get there.

Cosette emerged and let Abberline in while she dried her hair, which was a meticulous process of brushing, hair mousse and hairspray, before letting the products dry and putting in a headband. While she was doing this, Abberline sat himself on the couch only for Magnolia the cat to try and sit in his lap. He began to sneeze violently, and tried to move it away but the cat only followed him wherever he went.

"Did I feed Magnolia?" Cosette muttered to herself as she hurried about, stuffing her things into her purse and shaking her hands as she thought. "I did feed the cat. No, I didn't. Did I feed you?"

She stopped, giving the creature an inquiring look.

The ugly creature meowed in answer to the question. Cosette checked in the garbage bin where she found an empty can of cat-food.

"Ah, good, I did. Alright, we can go now," she said to Abberline.

❀❀❀

Agent Abberline stopped at a Dairy Queen that wasn't too far from the jail after hearing Cosette remark that she had never been to one. Cosette ordered a simple cheeseburger and fries, but was very keen on the idea of an ice cream blizzard. When they had both ordered, they found a table and sat in silence until they were called to come get their meal.

When they were seated comfortably they ate in silence. The director noticed that Cosette ate very sparingly, pausing every now and again to pick at her food ponderingly, as if hungry but hesitant to eat.

"So, how many cases have you actually called in about?" Abberline asked.

"Twenty-seven and a half," Cosette remarked without looking up.

"Why twenty-seven and a half? What's the half?"

"Well, that one was already half solved. It was the drug

deal In Las Vegas and L.A run by that Mic McKagen guy. It was all over the news. You see, they had Mic, who dealt in Nevada, but not his partner who dealt in California. They didn't know who the other guy was. Now, this one was rather intriguing because there wasn't much to go off of, and obviously, I didn't have the means to get across the states to look into it myself, nor was I licensed to look into such things personally. I noticed that one of the 'witnesses' going on trial, Terry Scotts, knew *way* too much about the drug deal for someone who had just 'seen it happen'. So I did a whole lot of digging online and offline—and don't worry, it was all legal...well, most of it anyways...and found out what hotel he was staying in. I was certain I could catch him doing something that would prove his guilt."

"You stalked him?"

"No, I just followed him and watched him closely until he did something illegal, which he did sooner than I expected. I caught him meeting up with other gang members, discussing who would take over McKagen's deals now that he was incarcerated. I managed to record the conversation with my phone, called the police and told them everything I had found out and Scotts got arrested," Cosette said.

"Wow," the director said. "So, did you get a reward or something?"

"My reward is getting to write about them," Cosette replied.

"But you could get a lot of money out of it," Abberline remarked.

"Yeah, but it's not about the money for me really."

"So you turn all your experiences into stories?"

"Yes, the McKagen case is a Helenor Gray short story by the name of *Drugs 'N' Roses*."

"Why that name?"

"It's like Guns 'N' Roses. Duff McKagan was the backing vocalist for the band, duh."

"Oh, I see."

"I thought it was funny."

"No, it is," Abberline assured her.

"Well, it looks like you're done, we ought to get going," Cosette said.

"You still have half a meal left."

"Oh, I'll take it for the road," the girl said.

Chapter Eleven:

"Hello, Mr. Herrod," Cosette said, standing before the cell and crossing her arms.

"Hello there, Cosette," Herrod answered. "You've finally arrived."

"What do you want, Mr. Herrod?" the girl asked, tapping her fingers on her crossed arms.

"Well, these detectives have wanted to investigate me, but I told them I wouldn't talk to anyone but you."

"I know that bit," Cosette remarked. "Go ahead and talk then."

"Ah, not with those three around," Herrod replied, indicating the detectives and the director.

"If you could excuse us?" Cosette asked them.

"Of course, but if you try anything—" Creed began.

"What could I do behind these bars?" Herrod asked with feigned innocence.

So Cosette and Herrod were left alone. Det. Creed had reluctantly given the girl the victim's files. Cosette looked through them. Abberline had already discussed Creed and Everglow's discoveries on their way from the DQ to the jail, though she still wanted to check the facts.

"You know, I get the feeling that your friends doubt my guilt," Herrod remarked, resting his arms on the bars of the cell.

"That's because you didn't kill anyone," Cosette said, without looking up from the files. "Do any of these men look familiar?"

She handed the convict the file and watched him carefully as he flicked through them. He handed it back over after a moment and grinned.

"I've never seen any of these men in my life," he remarked.

Cosette sighed, taking back the file.

"But I think I figured it out. Why you want to be in jail, that is. You witnessed your wife's death, didn't you?"

"Of course, I committed the murder after all."

"That's not true at all, but you say that because taking the fall was the only way you could keep yourself alive," Cosette said. "After you witnessed Amanda's death, the Ripper was going to kill you. But you thought quickly. You said that you wouldn't tell anyone. In fact, you offered to take the fall for Amanda's murder so that the police would be thrown off his trail. You also assumed that the Ripper wouldn't be able to reach you in jail if he changed his mind and decided to murder you after all. But you realized he *could* kill you even if you were locked up. The only thing between you and death was your agreement with Crane. That's why you wouldn't tell them who the real killer was, despite that being your intent. So now you're stuck here, and it is very clear that you *want* to tell me who the Ripper is, but you *can't*."

Herrod grinned.

"Did you solve my riddle yet?"

"'What makes a crane like a red herring?' No, I haven't solved it yet, but I will," the girl replied certainly. "You don't have any more clues, do you?"

"That depends on the questions you ask," Herrod answered.

"Who is the killer?" Cosette asked.

"Which killer?"

"The one who killed Amanda Herrod."

"Me."

"We just got through with the fact that it wasn't you."

"Did we?"

"What about her finger?"

"Her finger?"

"Her middle finger was cut off when her corpse was found."

"Ah, yes, I cut it off."

"Why?"

"A trophy to commemorate her memory."

"Why?"

"Because I felt she deserved it."

Cosette wondered if perhaps the killer wanted to commemorate the victim? Almost as if he had some respect for them. Maybe he wasn't killing them maliciously—at least, not in his mind.

"Do you know what makes a crane like a red herring?" Herrod asked again.

"No, I don't," Cosette replied wearily. "And I take it you aren't going to be of any more help unless I know *exactly* which questions to ask."

"Goodbye, Miss Bordeaux," Herrod called as she exited.

"So, what did he say?" Det. Creed asked as soon as she came out.

"Well, it wasn't exactly what he *said*. He lies between his teeth, but he's awful at it. You see, Mr. Herrod wasn't the murderer, but the *witness*."

"So he knows who the killer is?" Det. Everglow asked.

"Who are you?" Cosette asked the unfamiliar detective.

"Oh, I'm Det. Eleanor Everglow," she introduced herself. "I'm Det. Creed's new partner. It's nice to meet you."

"I'm Cosette H. Bordeaux—the 'H' is for Helenor. Sort of like Eleanor, but not quite. My parents named me after the helenor blue morpho, which is, in fact, my favorite butterfly. By the way, I apologize in advance for your new partner. If you don't lose your sanity within a week, perhaps you ought to run the station yourself," the girl remarked.

"Just tell us what you found out," Creed growled, scowling

at her.

"This isn't proof-positive, but I speculate that Herrod walked in on the Ripper murdering his wife and realized that the only way he could survive and potentially catch the killer was to take the fall *for* him. He promised to go to jail in place of the Ripper in exchange for his life. The Ripper stabbed him so it would look like a suicide attempt and left, knowing his tracks would be covered. Herrod wants to tell us who the killer is, but he's already on thin ice with the Ripper, and if he gives us a straight answer, he's as good as dead. At least, that's how I'd write it."

"Did he say if any of the men in the file were the Ripper?" Agent Abberline asked.

"He said he didn't recognise any of the men."

"Was he lying though?" Det. Creed asked.

"No, he didn't know any of them," Cosette replied. "All he said was 'What makes a crane like a red herring?'"

"That's a strange riddle," Det. Everglow remarked. "Maybe the answer will reveal the identity of the Ripper?"

"That's what I thought," Cosette agreed.

"Then let's try to solve the riddle as well as interrogating the men just to be safe. Det. Creed, I'm putting you as head of the interrogations while I see if I can't get Herrod a session with Dr. Vale. I think that would help with the case. Det. Everglow, if you, Det. Knox, and Cosette—if you'd like—could work on solving the riddle," Abberline directed.

"Yes, sir," Det. Creed replied, with a curt nod.

"And of course I'll help," Cosette said. "This is going to make for a fascinating story!"

❀❀❀

Pandora Crestmont, followed by Conrad Finnigan, entered the prison.

Thomas Herrod straightened up upon their approach in interest.

"Hello, Mr. Herrod," Pandora said, flashing a white smile. "How would you like to make a reappearance in the paper?"

Chapter Twelve:

That afternoon, Cosette, Det. Everglow, and Det. Knox went to the library to try deciphering the riddle Thomas Herrod had given Cosette. Det. Everglow had been researching cranes on her laptop while Seymour and Cosette had searched for books that might have some relation to the topic. All they found, though, was information on the bird or the construction machine.

"We've been working on this riddle all afternoon!" Seymour groaned.

"Well, you didn't expect this to be easy, did you?" Det. Everglow replied.

"Can we try looking up the riddle?" Det. Knox suggested. "There may be an answer online."

"That's cheating," Cosette remarked as Det. Everglow typed the riddle into the search bar, but all that came up was the difference between "cranes and herrings".

"That's no good," Everglow said. "Any other ideas?"

"Aren't there cranes in folklore?" Cosette inquired.

"There are, in fact," Det. Everglow said. "I've read about them mostly in Chinese folklore, though they appear in other cultures' folklore as well."

Det. Everglow searched the internet for cranes in mythology and folklore while Cosette and Seymour looked through the books they had found pertaining to cranes in folklore.

"I found something," Cosette said suddenly. "In Chinese mythology, they represent longevity, wisdom, and transcendence and are associated with Taoist immortals who could turn into cranes. They also represent purity of the human spirit as well as the quest for enlightenment. They were also messengers of the gods and possessed healing powers."

"That doesn't seem to have anything to do with the Richmond Ripper," Det. Everglow said.

"What does a red herring represent?" Seymour asked.

"Well, I don't know about the fish, but in literature it's typically something or someone that distracts the protagonist from an important truth or leads them to mistakenly expect a particular outcome—oh," Cosette realized.

"What?" Det. Knox asked.

"This whole riddle was a red herring to keep us from focusing on the answer," Det. Everglow remarked, catching on.

"So, then, what's the answer we should be focusing on?" Det. Knox asked.

"I'm not quite sure yet," Cosette admitted.

"I've called every man whom I'll be interrogating," Det. Creed sighed, sitting down at his desk. "Two I shut down because they have already caught the killers. The other three should be in tomorrow, but honestly, I think they're all innocent."

"Then tell the chief you don't want to do it," Det. Everglow said.

"It's the concept of it," Creed said. "But I say we just stick little Miss Psychic in a room with them; I'm sure we'll get some answers."

"We probably would," Cosette agreed.

The head-detective glared at her.

"So what did you find out about the riddle?" he asked Everglow.

"Well, we found out that 'What makes a crane like a red herring?' is quite literally the red herring," the detective replied.

"So it was just to throw us off?"

"Basically. Herrod was directing us farther away from the killer."

"I'm not so sure," Cosette said. "Maybe he's directing us to the killer and away from him at the same time."

"That son of a bitch is making my head hurt," Det. Creed grumbled, tucking his hands behind his head.

"Well, I'm going to clock out for the day, guys," Det. Knox said, stretching. "All this riddle solving is making my head hurt."

"We should probably head out and try to get some rest too," Det. Everglow agreed.

Det. Creed put on his coat, and Cosette grabbed her bag.

"Cosette, how about I drive you home? I don't like the idea of you walking back in the dark," Det. Everglow offered.

"Oh, uh, that would be great, thanks," Cosette said.

So she and Cosette went out to her car together after bidding Seymor and Creed good night. Cosette slipped into Everglow's passenger seat and gave her the directions to her apartment complex. Everglow turned on her car and the radio began blasting a song by The Smiths.

"Oh, sorry about that. Not very professional of me," Everglow said, embarrassed.

"Oh, don't worry about it. I love this band," Cosette assured her.

"Really?"

"Yeah, my dad and I used to listen to them all the time before he died."

"Oh, I'm sorry," Everglow said.

"About what?"

"Your dad, of course."

"Why? You didn't kill them."

"Both of them are—?"

"Yeah, it was a car crash."

"How old were you?"

"Seven."

"So, you must live with your relatives now?"

"I lived with my aunt and uncle for a while."

"What happened?"

"They didn't like me much, so I left and came here."

"Oh," Det. Everglow said.

"But it's nice—living on my own. Well, I'm not on my own; I have a cat."

"Oh, I have a cat too. Her name is Agatha Doyle."

"Like the writers?"

"Yeah, exactly."

"Those are some of my favorites. They inspire my work."

"You're a writer?"

"Yes. I do some short stories, but I have a book out—*Scarlet Reckoning*. You know, I just got a box of the hard backs that I'm taking down to the bookstore tomorrow. Do you want one?"

"Oh, totally, I'd love to read it," Everglow replied.

When they reached Cosette's complex they parked and got out, and Cosette led her inside.

Jimmy at the front desk was smoking something strong and had his feet kicked up on the desk. He leaned forward when he saw the two enter and blew smoke up into the air in grey rings that floated above his head before evaporating.

"Hey, Cosette. Who is this lovely lady?" Jimmy from the front desk drawled.

"Shut up, Jimmy, she's with the police," Cosette snapped.

That shut Jimmy up and Everglow and Cosette took the elevator up to the seventh floor. She let them into her room and they were immediately met by the ugly cat, which Cosette proceeded to pick up.

"This is Magnolia. Abberline thinks she's ugly—he's allergic to cats anyway. He has to take shots for his allergies."

"Hi, Magnolia," Everglow said, petting the cat, who purred in return.

Cosette let the woman hold the cat while she went to her room and took a copy of her novel from inside a cardboard box that sat in the corner. She signed it and gave the book to the detective.

"I hope you enjoy it," Cosette said.

"I definitely will," Everglow said, setting the cat on the couch. "And if you ever need anything, here's my number so you can call me."

"Alright, thank you. Goodnight, detective," Cosette said.

"Goodnight," the detective returned as the girl shut the door after her.

❀❀❀

Cosette had stayed up late that night.

She didn't think that the riddle was a complete red herring so she continued to research cranes in myth and lore to see if they might have some clue to the killer.

When she woke up, it was 11:12. She had just missed the wishing hour, she thought to herself. That was the only thought she had before a wave of overwhelming nausea washed over her.

"Oh, no, not again," she muttered.

She got up and made her way to the bathroom leaning over the toilet bowl until she was certain she wouldn't be sick. She found that her hands were trembling and rubbed them together.

Just then, a butterfly landed on her shoulder.

It was black with a strange design on the wings almost like a human skull. Cosette swatted it away, recoiling, and retreated to the living room.

She tried to ignore it and went to the cupboard, taking out a mug and the hot chocolate mix and set some water to boil. She sat the mug down on the coffee table in the living room and went to sit down when she noticed something odd about the mirror hanging on the wall across the living room.

She stood and went slowly to it, gazing into the glass.

The mirror was covered in the horrid butterflies now, and she could just see her reflection through the flapping of their wings. It couldn't have been her reflection looking back at her though, for it was black like a shadow and wore a crown of dark flowers from which the butterflies alighted.

The butterflies fluttered from the mirror onto Cosette,

and she began to feel that she couldn't breathe as the butterflies blinded her eyes. She looked back at the reflection, which smiled back at her.

"Who are you?"

Whether it was called out by herself or the reflection she didn't know, but it was the last thing she heard before everything went black.

❀❀❀

Cosette woke with a gasp. She looked over at the clock on her bedside table and saw that it said 4:03. She got up feeling utterly confused. Magnolia followed her into the living room where she found the cold mug of cocoa and a package of open Oreos still sitting on the floor beside the couch. Shaking off the grogginess she felt, the girl showered, dressed, did her hair, and then ate a few of the Oreos from the package from the floor. She was just putting Magnolia's cat food in a bowl when her phone began to ring.

"Hello?" she answered.

"Cosette, do you get the *Richmond Exposée*?" Agent Abberline asked.

"No, why?" Cosette asked, setting the bowl of cat food down on the ground.

"Well, a certain Ms. Pandora Crestmont decided to poke her nose where it doesn't belong—again—and went to talk to Thomas Herrod herself."

"Oh, no, what did she do?" Cosette asked apprehensively.

"She published an article in the *Exposée* relating the story of Thomas Herrod's 'crime', entirely from his side of the story."

"Okay? That's not the worst thing that could have happened. Maybe she twisted the story a bit, but it doesn't affect us, right?"

"All Herrod did in the article was badmouth what Pandora labeled 'The Virginia Copycat', after Herrod claimed that the Ripper only copied *his* method."

"He's trying to draw out the real killer," Cosette remarked, her brow furrowing in concern.

"By pissing him off? He literally called the Ripper, and I quote, 'A sex glorifying son of a bitch, who can't even come up with an original way to murder the women he finds attractive.'"

"Well, that'll do it."

"If your theory about Herrod trying to avoid the Ripper by getting himself arrested is right, then why would he contradict it like this?"

Cosette said nothing.

"The Richmond Ripper is probably going to do something in retaliation to this, and it's probably going to be something big. The problem is, we still don't know who this guy is or what he's going to do next," Abberline said.

"He's going to follow his pattern, but it will probably be extreme."

"We can't give a police escort to every blonde haired, blue eyed woman in Virginia, you do realize that, right?" Agent Abberline remarked.

"Yes, I know that. Which means that we'll have to figure out the identity of the Richmond Ripper before he can kill anyone else."

"Do you have any ideas on how we could do that?" the director asked.

"Not currently," Cosette admitted.

"Then we're just going to have to wait," Abberline said. "Oh, and Dr. Carnifex is expecting you at four this evening. Go if you want to stay on this case."

Agent Abberline hung up and Cosette groaned, tossing her phone down on the couch before sitting down herself and rubbing her eyes. She then picked up her phone again, momentarily scrolling through Pinterest before staring ponderously at the wall for a while before standing, grabbing her purse and coat, and hurrying at the door.

She went directly to the offices of the *Richmond Exposée* and went to the chief editor's office. The chief editor was a fat, short, old man who looked as though he could have been in *The Great Muppet Caper*. He was smoking a cigar and reading the latest paper they had printed.

"I'd like to speak with Ms. Pandora Crestmont, please," Cosette remarked.

"Why?" the editor asked lazily.

"It's about the Richmond Ripper."

The editor raised his eyebrows.

"Don't you mean the Virginia Copycat?"

"Whatever. I just need to speak with her about her article."

"What's your name, kid?"

"Cosette. She'll remember me," the girl replied.

The editor disappeared down the hallway and came back a moment later to let Cosette know she could speak with Pandora Crestmont.

Cosette went back and found Pandora sitting at her desk, typing on her computer. The woman didn't bother to look up at her when she entered.

"Why did you put out the article about Herrod and the Ripper?" Cosette demanded to know.

"Someone needed to do it. The public wants the truth; I gave it to them," Pandora remarked without looking up.

"You gave them a lie they wanted to hear, not a truth that was any bit real," Cosette replied.

"Well, at least *I* gave them a story."

"Anyone can give them a story. They don't care. Look at them. They've started reading Wattpad fanfictions rather than actual novels. Though admittedly, I would too if your work was the other option."

"The feeling is mutual," Pandora replied.

"You do realize that the Ripper is going to read your article?" Cosette asked.

"I do hope so, and I'm sure you do too," Pandora remarked, shuffling papers on her desk.

"He's going to kill someone."

"All in the name of a story, right?" the woman smirked.

"I'd rather give them the astounding truth, rather than the fictitious lie. If they find it boring, then they clearly haven't the mind to conceive," Cosette returned sharply.

"So wise," Pandora said sarcastically. "But what do you want me to do about it?"

"I want you to write an article explaining that everything you said was just to draw the Ripper out," Cosette answered.

"Hmm…let me think…No," Pandora said.

"The FBI will make you."

"No, they won't, and I won't be doing anything to withdraw my article."

"Then simply know that whatever happens next, blood is on your hands."

"Then I'll simply wash it off," Pandora returned.

Chapter Thirteen:

Dr. Adlea Vale was escorted down the halls to a room that was most likely used for interrogations. There were two small, barred windows that let in light besides a fluorescent light that hung above the table where Thomas Herrod was sitting, handcuffed.

He looked smugly at her as she entered and set her attachè case down, sitting across from the man.

"Hello again. I'm Dr. Adlea Vale. You may remember me from the first time Cosette visited you."

"So, first the FBI sent a little girl to interrogate me, and now they've put me in counseling," Herrod smiled, leaning forwards in his chair and folding his hands on the table.

"I'm not here for counseling," Dr. Vale said. "I'm just here to talk. We want to know what you witnessed during your wife's murder."

"Witnessed? No, I murdered her."

Dr. Vale raised an eyebrow and hummed in disbelief.

"Well, then, shall we begin?" she asked.

"Whenver you like," Herrod replied.

"You said you didn't have a good relationship with Amanda, is that right?" the doctor began.

"Yes, that's right," Herrod nodded.

"How so?"

"Well, I suppose every woman has her flaws, but Amanda seemed to have more than other women. She wasn't like this at first, when we met, but after we were engaged she began to show signs of narcissism. We got married but all she ever did was yap. I couldn't do a damn thing right for the woman. We used to scream and holler at each other, we broke plates and cups and all sorts of things. Well, she stormed out one night and didn't come back. This started happening a lot. Little did I know she was cheating on me.

"God, when I found out, that was the last straw. We had a good long fight, and then I grabbed the knife out of the carving block. Oh, she loved me then. Told me how much she loved me and how she was sorry she had cheated on me. But she was only saying that so I'd spare her life. She didn't mean a thing of it. So I stabbed her to death."

"Hm," Dr. Vale nodded. "It can be very upsetting to have someone that close to you betray you."

"Yes, very much. I think about it all the time."

"Do you think that people like that, unfaithful spouses and such, ought to die?"

"I think it should warrant the death penalty. Too bad I had to carry out justice myself," Herrod said, leaning back in his chair.

"So you don't feel guilty for killing her?"

"Not at all."

"Why would you cut off her finger then? If you hated her so much, I mean," Dr. Vale said.

"I don't hate her. I've never hated her. I loved her. That's why her actions were so hard for me to fathom. I cut off her finger, I suppose, for the same reason that the Victorians used to cut off bits of their lover's hair and keep it in a locket. I wanted to have a piece of her with me, even if she was underground. Even if she didn't love me, I still loved her."

Dr. Vale nodded.

"It's nearly romantic," she said, gauging his reaction.

He paused, studying her. "Exactly."

"Why do you think you don't feel any remorse for killing your wife?'

"She did something horrible. Like I said, it merited exactly what I gave her."

"So in your mind, it's justifiable?"

"Absolutely."

Dr. Vale paused for a moment and inspected the convict's face.

"You look sad when you talk about your wife," she remarked.

"Of course I do. She hurt me. Haven't you ever been hurt, Doctor?"

"Emotions are universal. It is our response to them that defines who we are as people," the woman nodded.

"So you understand, then, the pain that I feel?"

"Perhaps not your exact pain, but I can empathize with you. The thing I don't understand is why you couldn't have let the courts take care of it."

"What do you mean?"

"A divorce."

Herrod looked at his feet as if contemplating the ground.

"I didn't want a divorce. I wanted her to be my wife."

"Does it hurt any less now?"

"I don't think so," Herrod said.

"Do you miss her?"

"Very much."

"Even after the way she treated you?"

"Well, I don't think I miss *that* particular part of her," Herrod chuckled.

Suddenly, an alarm rang signaling that their time was up.

"Well, that's all the time we have for today," Dr. Vale said, checking her watch as she stood and took up her bag. "I look forward to our next session."

"It was a pleasure to talk to you," Herrod agreed, grinning as the guard came in to return him to his cell.

"Oh, and one last thing, Mr. Herrod," Dr. Vale paused and

turned back around to face him.

"Yes, Doctor?"

"Cosette was right. You are an awful liar."

❀❀❀

When Dr. Vale had finished her session with Thomas Herrod, she went down to the station to meet the Abberlines and relate all Herrod had said.

"We were wondering when you would come in," Chief Abberline greeted her. "My husband is in my office with my detectives."

Agent Abberline was sitting in one of the chairs in front of the desk bending over a chess board they had set up while Cosette was sitting on the desk watching amusedly as he pondered his next move.

"I have him in check," Cosette chuckled.

"Really?" the chief asked, smiling and bending over her husband's shoulder. "You never lose at chess."

"I may this time around," the director laughed. "She's not bad."

"Can we put this up and focus on the case?" Det. Creed asked irritatedly.

"Hold on," Agent Abberline said, making his move.

Cosette's next move won her the game, and she cleaned it away as the two detectives, the chief, and the doctor settled themselves around the desk.

Dr. Vale related what had been told to her by Herrod and when she was finished, Chief Abberline sighed.

"It's the exact same conversation we had before," Creed groaned.

"This is hopeless. This guy thinks he's so funny. I'll show him funny when I crack his jaw—"

"That's violent," Everglow chided him.

"That's the point," Creed returned.

"This is not the same story Mr. Herrod told us the first time," Cosette remarked thoughtfully.

"What do you mean?" the chief asked.

"Mr. Herrod never said his wife cheated on him."

"He seems very withdrawn. He might've been withholding it until he felt safer talking about it," Det. Everglow said. "Or maybe he thought we already knew his reasoning."

"That was his reasoning in court as well," Creed said.

"He told me he killed her because she was annoying," Cosette remarked. "I think he's editing his story every time he has to tell it to make it more plausible."

"And how is this going to help us find the Ripper?" Det. Creed asked.

"It might not help us find him, but it may help us know what Mr. Herrod witnessed."

"So, if we take away his alleged lie about his wife cheating on him, everything he told us was what he walked into the day the Ripper murdered his wife," Det. Everglow remarked.

"Exactly. Did Herrod seem like he was lying about anything else?" Cosette asked.

"He's clearly very still in love with his wife for one thing."

"It's clear he hated lying about killing her. He hates people thinking he killed her, and he hates the Crane for what he's done," Cosette said.

"So, from what he said, it seems that the Ripper broke in, cut Amanda Herrod's throat and was cutting her finger off when Herrod walked in," Det. Creed laid out. "Then the Ripper stabs Herrod, but why let him live?"

"So that he wouldn't get caught, just as Herrod said," Det. Everglow said.

"But there's a fifty percent chance Herrod would spill to the cops anyways," Creed replied.

"Maybe he didn't want to kill him because he didn't fit the pattern," Cosette mused. "And because Herrod promised to take responsibility for the Ripper's actions."

"So why stab him anyway?" the chief asked.

"I think it was a threat," Cosette said. "That if he told, he'd come and kill Herrod."

"So that's why he can't tell us anything," the chief added.

"Right."

"But he can give us clues," Det. Everglow said. "It's a loophole."

"He said we had to solve the clues he already gave us before he gives us more," Cosette reminded them.

"Well, then we'd better get to solving before the Ripper strikes again," Agent Abberline remarked.

Chapter Fourteen:

"Goodbye, Gustav. I'll have Judith put in a refill for you at once," Dr. Carnifex remarked as he showed his patient out.

He went and spoke with his secretary momentarily before turning to Cosette who was sitting on the lobby sofa.

"Come along, my dear," he said, and led her to his office.

He sat down and took up his notebook. Crossing one leg over the other, he watched Cosette as she examined the glass figurines in one of the cases.

"So, what's on your mind today, Cosette?" Dr. Carnifex asked her.

She paused in her work at alphabetically reordering his bookcases and tilted her head to one side.

"A lot of things," she replied.

"Like what?"

"Like why do you take off your wedding ring before you come into work?"

"My wedding ring?"

Cosette hummed.

"You have a mark on your ring finger that indicates you were wearing a ring not too long ago."

"Yes, I only wear it to bed," Dr. Carnifex replied, examining his hand.

"Is it because you miss her?"

"My wife?"

"Yes, how did she die?"

Dr. Carnifex raised an eyebrow.

"And who is to say she died?"

"Are you divorced?"

"No."

"Well, the only other options are that you're cheating or that your wife is dead," Cosette remarked.

The doctor was quiet for a moment.

"Yes, she died. She was murdered."

"By whom?"

"We don't know," the doctor admitted.

"We?"

"Arnold attempted to help me solve her case. That is how I met him. We never did catch the killer though. In return for his assistance, I helped him on two different cases that required a psychologist. But I do think he's quite forgotten her case by now."

"Why don't you ask him to reopen the case?" the girl asked.

"Because he never closed it. There just isn't any evidence to catch the murderer. We don't even know why she was killed. In fact, Abberline said it was one of the hardest cases he's ever seen next to the Richmond Ripper case," Dr. Carnifex answered.

"How intriguing," Cosette remarked, returning to her arranging. "I do hope it gets solved."

The doctor chuckled.

"As do I."

The office then fell quiet as Dr. Carnifex watched Cosette finish with one bookcase and begin on another.

"Well, I haven't anything else to say," Cosette remarked finally. "So I think I'll take my leave."

"Or we could see this session through," the doctor remarked.

"Well, I want to go work on my story and quite possibly the Ripper case," Cosette said. "Now, if you'll excuse me—"

"I will not. Now, I'm going to set this timer for the remaining forty-five minutes we have, and you will tell me whatever else comes to your mind that you think ought to be discussed in a session. Remember, without these sessions, there is no case for you."

Cosette humphed but returned to rearranging the books.

"So, what else is on your mind, Cosette?"

"You don't happen to know what makes a crane like a red herring, do you?" Cosette asked.

"I'm afraid I don't," the doctor said after some thought.

"I didn't think so," Cosette said, setting aside another Sir Arthur Conan Doyle novel.

They sat in a silence that seemed to be awkward for Cosette alone before the doctor inquired, "May I ask why you look so tired?"

"Well, to be frank, Doctor, my sleep has lately been plagued by my own mind," the girl answered coldly.

"You've been having nightmares?" Dr. Carnifex asked, scribbling in his notebook.

"That's what I said."

"Only nightmares?"

"Well, I have sleep paralysis—or rather, sleep hallucinations—and then I wake up having walked about in my sleep."

"What are they about, may I ask?"

"Butterflies. It's always these black butterflies. And this darkness…"

"Darkness?"

"Yes, and it looks like…a human."

"Do you recognize the person this 'darkness' portrays?"

"No," Cosette said after a beat of silence.

The doctor nodded, looking up from his notepad.

"I think it would be wise to perhaps prescribe you some medication, at least for your sleep."

"Oh, no, I don't want medication," Cosette declined.

"And why would that be?"

"The last time I was on drugs I got the extreme symptoms: loss and gain of weight, worsened depression and anxiety, random bleeding, ecceterra."

"Well, then I will simply have to look into your medical and therapeutic history to find a prescription right for you. Do you have any names of your old therapist?"

"Well, there was Dr. Sarah Mallard, and, boy, was she a bad psychiatrist! Once her son almost killed himself over the phone during one of the sessions, and she didn't even bother to leave the room; I heard the whole thing."

Cosette stopped to chuckle to herself, though the doctor raised his eyebrows in concern.

"Perhaps that affected you negatively?" he asked.

"I don't know," the girl shrugged. "But after Mallard there was...Emma Somebody-Or-Other and she was brand new in the field and used 'animal-therapy,' but my aunt and uncle pulled me when she said she might have to get the government involved with my situation."

"Were your aunt and uncle abusive towards you?"

"I wouldn't say *that*...But you know the Dursleys from *Harry Potter*?"

"I do," the doctor nodded.

"They were basically them. I've even got a cousin who's an asshole. He's really skinny though, not like Dudley. But back to the point. After that there was Dr. Greta Martin and she was *nuts*. She thought I was possessed by a demon or something."

"Are your aunt and uncle religious?"

"Not really, they just didn't like me very much," Cosette said. "But anyway, I'd just recommend talking to Dr. Adlea Vale since she recommended you to Abberline for me."

"Is that all of your references?"

"Dr. Vale is my only reference."

"Alright. Do you have a medical doctor?"

"Not currently, but I did in Vermont. Dr...Sherry Willams, I think."

"Very good then," the doctor said, closing his notebook just as the timer on his phone went off. "Ah, it seems we have successfully made it through the entire session. I should applaud you. And I must thank you as well for rearranging my bookshelves. I will look forward to the finishing of your organization during our next session. I should have thought to organize them alphabetically before."

But Cosette didn't hear him. She was staring, wide eyed, at the book in her hands. It was titled *The Monster and Other Stories* by Steven Crane.

"Cosette?" Dr. Carnifex asked when she didn't respond.

"Thank you for the session, Doctor, I've got to go!" Cosette exclaimed, grabbing her bag and sprinting out the door before the doctor could say another word.

Chapter Fifteen:

Cosette ran all the way to the police station and was quite disheveled when she reached Det. Everglow's desk.

"Cosette? What are you doing here?" Everglow asked in surprise.

"What makes a crane like a red herring?" Cosette asked, trying to catch her breath.

"Oh, God, not this stupid riddle again," Det. Creed groaned, coming to sit down at his desk.

"Go ahead, Cosette," Everglow said.

"The lowercase 'c' in 'crane'. Crane isn't a bird or a metaphor, it's a *person*!"

"We've got to tell the chief," Det. Everglow remarked excitedly, standing from the desk at once.

The three hurriedly went across to Chief Abberline's office, where she and her husband had been discussing another case.

"What's going on?" asked Chief Abberline as they burst in.

"Cosette may have just solved the stupid riddle Herrod gave her," Creed replied. "Crane's a person."

"Our killer?" Chief Abberline asked.

"Herrod laid it out for us on a silver platter," the head-detective said.

Everglow began typing mercilessly at her laptop for less than three minutes and then exclaimed, "There's a Crane from

Virginia, but only one. Draven Crane."

She turned the picture around for the others to see. The other four hurried around her to see the photo of a middle aged man, with blond, closely cropped hair and icy blue eyes. He didn't look like a killer. He was rather handsome actually.

"His wife was even murdered *exactly* according to the pattern and way before the other victims. There's just one problem," Det. Everglow said.

"And that would be?" Det. Creed asked.

"He's been dead for ten years."

"What?" the others cried.

"Apparently he was in a boating accident. He went fishing, and the gas line leaked. It blew up right after his wife, Nora Crane, was murdered."

"That sounds like Fake Your Death 101," Cosette remarked.

"That's probably because it was," Det. Creed agreed.

"Alright, I'm going to have you three find out everything you can about this Draven Crane because I get the feeling that he isn't dead, and he's our Ripper," Chief Abberline ordered. "Cosette, you can help if you want, though you've already done more than enough."

"Actually, I'd like to visit Mr. Herrod again. He said he would tell me more if I solved his riddle," Cosette said.

"Oh, brilliant. I'll have someone take you down," Abberline replied.

"Actually, there's something I need to talk to you about," she told the director.

"Alright," Abberline said.

He had to put his work away, grabbed his phone off his wife's desk and led the girl to his car.

"So, what did you want to tell me?"

"I want you to reopen Dr. Carnifex's case," Cosette said.

"His case?" Abberline asked.

"He told me about it last session when I realized that she was dead. His wife was murdered, and you promised to help solve the case,"

"God, I forgot about that completely," Abberline said sheepishly. "But we never closed that case."

"Yeah, you just forgot all about it," Cosette grumbled.

"We had no evidence at all on who killed them. We couldn't do anything about it. There were no fingerprints, no DNA, no sign that anyone had been there except the corpses."

"Wait…there were multiple corpses?" Cosette asked in surprise.

"He didn't tell you about his daughter?"

"No."

"Jenephie Carnifex was murdered as well."

Cosette was quiet at the realization, finding that she was rather startled by the matter.

"I didn't know he had children. How old was she?"

"She was ten. And this was six years ago. She would be your age now," Abberline said. "Look, Cosette, believe you me, if I could solve that case, I would. But there is nothing we could use to trace the killer, especially now."

When they arrived at the jail, Abberline and Cosette went inside, though the director waited in the hallway outside knowing that Herrod wouldn't talk unless Cosette alone was in the room.

"Well, hello again. Back so soon?" Herrod asked when he saw her enter.

"I solved your riddle," Cosette remarked.

"Did you? Pray do tell the answer," Herrod said, cupping his ear theatrically.

"The word 'crane' was both the red herring *and* the answer. We knew that the riddle was a red herring in and of itself, but we thought that the word 'crane' would prove some importance in the matter. Of course, it did. We just thought it meant something else—a bird, for instance, or a metaphor. But Crane is a person. Draven Crane to be exact. You gave us the exact information we needed. We just couldn't see it."

Herrod's face contorted strangely into something close to

a smile and a concerned frown at the same time.

"So it *is* him. He isn't dead, is he? You saw him alive the night he killed Amanda Herrod."

"I think you're too smart for your own good, Miss Bordeaux," Herod replied.

"You do not how many times I've been told that, Mr. Herrod. Now do you have any other clues for me?"

"You're very enthusiastic. Got any paper?"

Cosette hurriedly extracted her notebook and a pencil. Herrod took it from her and scribbled something onto the paper and handed it back to her. Cosette examined it and found it was an address.

"Mummy dearest can tell you more about the Crane than I can," Herrod said. "Tell her that Tom sent you, and ask her what she found under the pear tree."

"Is that all?" Cosette asked.

"Yes," Herrod said in a tone that conveyed that he was done with the conversation.

"Thank you," Cosette said. "Oh, and one more thing. Why did you agree to do the interview with Pandora Crestmont?"

"The exact reason you think I did it. I wanted to draw Crane out. I don't care much for my life anymore to be honest. Crane took the one thing I loved, and now I'm taking the blame for his sin. I only framed myself for this so that I could eventually attempt to catch him and see him put to justice. But I think I'm about tired of trying to think up a way to survive and reveal the real killer. So, I thought I'd help you out a little."

Cosette nodded her understanding and replaced her notebook in her bag. As she exited to meet with Abberline, she accidentally bumped into one of the guards, who was going the opposite way.

"Oh, my goodness, I'm so sorry!" Cosette remarked.

"It's quite alright, Miss," the guard assured her, tipping his hat.

As Cosette left, she couldn't shake the strange feeling she had gotten from the guard. He had seemed too simple, too unnoticeable, too normal. She was sure she knew him from somewhere, but she wasn't familiar with any middle aged, tan, brunet men.

"That guard was strange," Cosette told Abberline.

"Seemed nice to me," the director said. "What did Herrod say?"

"He gave me this," the girl said, showing him the notebook.

"An address?"

"Yes, and the address of Crane's mother at that. He said to 'Tell her that Tom sent her and to ask her what was under the pear tree.'"

"Well, that's an odd revelation. I'll call the others at once."

❀❀❀

When they arrived at Mrs. Crane's house, they went up the front steps and the chief rapped on the door. At first, no one answered, but upon knocking a few more times an older woman answered without removing the chain. She had tousled, fading blonde hair and dull, blue eyes, staring out nervously at them.

"Hello?" she asked.

"Hello, I'm Chief Abberline of the Virginia Police Department and this is Det. Creed and Det. Everglow, and Agent Abberline, director of the BAU," the chief remarked.

The woman looked suspiciously at the badges they procured.

"What do you want?" she asked worriedly.

"Tom sent us," Cosette said. "Can you tell us what you found under the pear tree?"

The woman sighed deeply and shut the door back with a sharp click. The five all exchanged confused glances before they heard the woman undo the chain, stepping back to let them in.

The house they stepped into was rather bland and simple, set up rather like those Ikea showrooms. Mrs. Crane didn't bother opening the curtains and blinds. She seemed very out of it, a half-smile twisting her vacant eyes.

"Why don't you sit down? Would you like some tea?" Mrs.

Crane asked.

"No, thank you," Det. Everglow declined.

"You seem rather calm. Have you been expecting this?" Cosette asked.

"Who are you?" Mrs. Crane asked, eyeing the girl uncertainly.

"I'm Cosette Bordeaux," Cosette answered.

"She's with us unfortunately," Det. Creed said.

"Well, I figured you would be coming around here sooner or later," Mrs. Crane sighed, pouring herself a cup of tea and sitting down.

"Your son is Draven Crane, correct?" Agent Abberline made certain.

"Yes, that's right."

"Do you know that he's killed people?" Det. Creed asked.

"Yes, I did. I figured that one out for myself."

"And you never thought to tell the police?"

"Well, I couldn't," she paused coyly and redirected. "But, tell me, how do you know Tom?"

"His case was too similar to the other Ripper cases, and we looked into it. He gave me the strangest riddle, 'What makes a crane like a red herring?' I solved it, and it led me to the realization that the killer's *name* was Crane. We found out his wife had in fact been murdered by the Ripper," Cosette said. "When I told him I had solved the riddle, he told us to come here to see you."

"I see," Mrs. Crane nodded and stood. "Give me a moment."

Mrs. Crane left the living room and went upstairs for a minute.

"You don't think she would try to escape out the window, do you?" Det. Creed asked in an undertone.

"That would definitely make for an interesting couple of chapters," Cosette replied.

"I think she's a bit too much of an airhead to try that," Agent Abberline added.

The woman was gone for several minutes and Det. Creed was just thinking about going to check on the old woman when they heard her footsteps on the stairs. Mrs. Crane re-entered carrying an envelope. She sat down again, nervously rubbing the envelope between her fingers. She handed it over to Chief Abberline. The chief opened it and extracted a piece of folded paper. She unfolded it, and her face contorted into a disgusted frown.

The others leaned over to look at what she held and saw that it was a demented picture of a singular, severed finger lying in an open wooden cigar box in a hole of moist dirt under the pear tree.

"So, that's the finger of Nora Miller," Mrs. Crane said, tapping the picture. "Or rather Nora *Crane*."

"He's guilty because he killed his wife," Det. Everglow remarked suddenly. "That's why Cosette said the crimes were remorseful."

"Nora, she always loved plants. She planted the pear tree out back for my birthday when it was just a little sprout. But that was eleven years ago, before Nora was killed," Mrs. Crane said, waving her hand. "He faked his death, you know. I figured it out. I believe it was because he was afraid the police would figure out that he had killed Nora. Of course, they wouldn't be wrong. I suppose I never *was* really the best mother and he *has* been through so much, I just wanted to help him to make up for it all so I kept quiet about him faking his death.

"Six years ago, I found the finger while trying to plant some flowers under the tree. I panicked and didn't know what to do so I tried calling his old number and left a message saying that I had found something under the pear tree. I took several pictures of the box while I waited for a response. I had planned on sending them to the police. But he called me back and told me that if I brought any of the evidence to the police I would be arrested for accessory to murder. He said that he would come take it from me. I didn't want to get arrested or anything so I just gave it to him. He burnt most of the photos except for this one, which I managed to save. I guess I always knew the police would come for us.

"It wasn't long before I heard about murder after murder

just like Nora's," Mrs. Crane sighed, shrugging her shoulders. "I figured that Draven was the one they called 'The Richmond Ripper.' Then I heard about the murder of Amanda Herrod. They said that her husband, Thomas Herrod had killed her, but I didn't believe it for one second. I knew it wasn't Tom who had killed his wife. She had died the same way Nora had been murdered. So, after he had been incarcerated, I went to talk with him personally.

"When I told him who I was and why I had come, he told me exactly everything that had happened. He said that he had been late home from work and stopped for take out and flowers for Amanda on his way home to surprise his wife with a dinner date. When he got home he was just in time to witness Draven stabbing his wife to death.

"He was scared out of his mind, but thought quickly. He promised Draven that he would take the fall for the murder if he let him live. Draven was desperate and knew that killing Tom could ultimately ruin him in the long run if he broke off his pattern. He agreed and stabbed Tom to make it look like a murder-suicide, then he went to jail in Draven's place.

"Tom even told me his idea about exposing Draven, but said that I couldn't tell anyone until he came up with a plan, so I didn't tell anyone," Mrs. Crane said.

"Has Crane had any contact with you lately?" Agent Abberline asked.

"Of course not. He's supposed to be dead, remember?"

"But you don't really believe that, do you?" asked Det. Creed.

"I think he wanted to fake his death," Mrs. Crane answered. "So that he would be apprehended by the police and so he could kill more freely." Mrs. Crane sighed softly here. "This is all my fault. You know, Draven's father was so abusive to him. He used to shout at him, beat him, sometimes so badly he couldn't go to school. I always stepped aside, selfishly afraid that I would be harmed myself. I suppose I didn't want to see any of it at the time. I didn't want to acknowledge it. Acknowledgement gives way to blame, and blame gives way to guilt. Over time, Draven grew depressed, anxious, and would have extreme paranoia because of his father's abuse, which would even lead to nightmares or hallucinations. Of course, this brought even more abuse to him. It was a ruthless cycle.

"School was no better. He was mercilessly bullied for his quietness and the obvious injuries from his father. I never bothered to take him to a psychologist for any of this because I was afraid that we might be split up and I would lose Draven to his father in court or even Protective Services. He graduated high school and went off to college where he stopped speaking to us all together.

"I think the worst of it was when Draven had to come home from school because of how bad his mental health got. Obviously, his father did nothing in the way of helping him heal. Just a little before he came home he had met Nora at school, and they eventually started dating. During his break from college she tried to come over a few times, but Draven would always send her home as soon as possible. He was afraid that his father would find out about her and try to bring some harm to her as well just as he did to him. Things had just gotten so much worse and he was more afraid of his father than ever. His worst fears came true when his father finally found out about Nora after going through Draven's phone one day.

"When he was angry or drunk, which was most of the time, he used to threaten Draven that he would harm or even kill Nora. I knew they were empty threats, but Draven didn't. Draven eventually went back to college after a few months of his father's abuse and never saw his father again—my husband died drunk-driving.

"Nora, though, was the sweetest girl I had ever known. She was the one who convinced Draven to visit me again so she could meet me. He did return during the Christmas holidays to introduce us to each other properly, but I don't think our relationship ever healed. How could it with all that I had let happen to him? He seemed far better mentally than he had before, though, thanks to Nora.

"But some time after their marriage, Draven began to get paranoid again. He would call me late at night or in the early hours of the morning in a panic talking incoherently about his father saying that he heard banging around the house like someone breaking in. His things would go missing. He stopped taking his prescription because he was certain it was being replaced with poison by whomever was breaking into his house—he was determined it was his father trying to kill him. He seemed to have forgotten that his father was dead, and he never believed anything else. The next thing I knew, Nora had been killed," Mrs. Crane finished.

"My question is, why would he bury Nora's finger in your backyard?" the chief asked. "That doesn't make any sense."

"Maybe he wanted to leave it as a gift before he faked his death, or perhaps an apology for what he had done and what he was going to do."

"No, that isn't it at all," Cosette spoke up, examining a clothing magazine that sat on the coffee table. "It was an accusation."

"What?" Mrs. Crane asked.

"It was an accusation. He was saying 'Look at what you made me. Look at what I have become.' He's blaming you for Nora's death. He can't accept what he's done. He just never expected you to actually find it. It was just there for his own personal comfort."

"And that's why he keeps killing," Det. Creed added. "Because the abuse and the guilt drove him insane, and when he sees anyone who looks like Nora, he panics and has to kill her."

"It's like something out of an Edgar Allan Poe story," Det. Everglow remarked.

"Can you tell us where he went to school and where he lived after he moved out?"

"He went to Richmond High and graduated from the University of Maryland in Baltimore with a psychology degree. I'll find the address of his old house if you'll give me a moment."

Mrs. Crane went out of the room again and returned with a piece of paper, on which she had written out the needed address and handed it to the chief.

"If you do call the schools though, I'm not sure anyone would even know who you're talking about. He never had any friends, and not even the teachers knew him. I think that if they had they might have done something to help him. I wish they had," Mrs. Crane sighed.

"Thank you for your cooperation, Mrs. Crane," the chief remarked. "We'll call you if we need anything else."

"And I would recommend you don't leave town," Agent Abberline warned.

❀❀❀

"I just called the college and his old high school, and they actually had to *look him up* to know who I was talking about," Det. Creed remarked. "They didn't even know what he looked like when I gave him Crane's description. This guy was a total nobody."

"So how are we supposed to find him?" Det. Everglow asked. "I mean, he's legally dead, which makes this situation a lot harder for us."

Suddenly, Cosette's phone began to ring, and she excused herself and hurriedly answered it when she saw the caller.

"Hello, Mr. Bedford?...Today?...I completely forgot...Yes, I do have the new novel in progress, but it won't be finished for what seems like a while yet...No, I don't know how long...Well, I have another short story for the *Helenor Gray* series, so I'll just send you that...Alright, I'll email it to you as soon as I get home... Yes, Mr. Bedford, I *do* leave my house—on occasion...I'm at the police station...Yes, I'm still on the case..." the girl chuckled at something being said. "Alright...Okay...Bye-bye."

She then returned to Det. Creed and Det. Everglow's desk.

"Trouble?" Det. Creed asked, without looking up.

"I've got to get home. My newspaper's editor-in-chief wants something in by tonight."

"Alright, see you later, Cosette," Det. Everglow said.

Cosette took her leave from the station, though as she made her way home in the dimming evening, she couldn't help but look around herself for she couldn't shake the feeling that something or someone was watching her, but the only people around were a group of pedestrians waiting to cross the street, waiting to cross. So, she continued to her apartment.

As she reached the door of the apartment, she noticed that someone had moved into the room across from her own. She wondered who it was. Probably someone pretty desperate. She was aware this apartment building wasn't ideal. Still, the seventh floor was even less ideal than the other parts of the complex since it had the most issues, thus being cheaper than the other apartments, and Cosette's ability to afford it.

She wasn't quite sure why she thought so hard about someone else moving in on her floor. Perhaps it perturbed her slightly. Perhaps it was her hatred for change, or perhaps she had simply enjoyed having the whole of the seventh floor to herself. But nevermind any of that, she had to email her short story to Mr. Bedford if she wanted her paycheck.

Chapter Sixteen:

Cosette hadn't heard from the Virginia Police Department or the FBI in a few days since they had talked with Mrs. Crane. She only had Det. Everglow's number and the Abberlines' numbers and she felt she shouldn't call either of the Abberlines unless it was an emergency and Everglow was probably busy.

She went to the store for groceries while she was "off-duty" from the police and FBI. While she was out, she picked up a few things for baking, more out of boredom than necessity, and made cookies. She thought it might be nice to share some of the cookies with her new neighbor, whoever they were. It was the kind of gesture she would have appreciated when she moved in —if anyone had even known she was there.

She had a bit of a tendency to be a ghost. In fact, no one in the complex knew she lived there—except for Jimmy, of course. And there was one night guard who she often said hello to when she came in from being out late.

She spent the afternoon baking and working on the latest chapter of her book. She carried a notebook with her everywhere, and she would always write down everything that happened involving the case in her free time. Later, she would convert it into a chapter of her new novel. She tapped her pencil idly on the desk, frowning as she paused her work on the computer to try and think up a title for her novel, which she still didn't have.

When the cookies had come out of the oven, she decorated them and put as many as she could fit in a tupperware with a homemade card that read: "*Welcome To The Building*! *Sincerely, Your Neighbor*." She left it outside the closed door.

The next day, around lunch, her phone began to ring. When she looked at the caller, she saw it was Agent Abberline. She hurriedly answered it.

"Cosette, we did some digging and uncovered Draven Crane's old house that he moved into after killing Nora. The location was confirmed by Mrs. Crane. We'd like you to come and just see if you pick up on anything we missed."

"You do realize I just woke up like thirty minutes ago, right?" Cosette grumbled.

"Why are you so upset? Weren't you the one who was so thrilled to assist in a 'real-life mystery' in the first place?"

"I *am* thrilled, I'm just tired," Cosette remarked. "And your lovely Dr. Carnifex doesn't help with my sleep issues all that much."

"That's because you don't *let* him help you. I think you might have some trouble with letting people help you."

Cosette rolled her eyes and agreed to come down, hung up and put on her coat. Agent Abberline had texted her the address of the house. It was all the way in the next town over and she didn't have a car. Though she recalled that, at one point Seymour Knox had given her his number "in case she ever needed anything."

"Hey, Cosette!" Seymour answered when she called. "What's up?"

"Abberline asked me to come check out the old home of Draven Crane. It's in the next town over, and I haven't got a car, so could you accompany me?" Cosette asked.

"No problem. I'll be over in a bit."

Seymour picked her up in front of her building and drove her to Crane's house. It was a small bungalow that was rather secluded from the neighborhood by trees and several acres.

Agent and Chief Abberline, Det. Creed and Det. Everglow were talking to the owners of the house in the front yard. Seymour parked by the sidewalk, and they got out.

"Cosette, you finally arrived. Hello, Det. Knox," Agent Abberline greeted them.

"What did you find out so far?" Cosette inquired.

"This is Mr. And Mrs. Hopkins. They rent the house now and said we could search the place for evidence even though they didn't think we would find anything."

"Well, did you?" Cosette asked.

"Not yet."

"Have you ever heard the name Draven Crane?" Cosette asked the old couple.

"Mr. Abberline here asked us about someone by that name," Mrs. Hopkins answered.

"Nevermind that then. Have you searched the place already?" Cosette asked the director.

"Yes, while we waited for you, though we wanted you to look around just in case, like I said over the phone."

"May I see inside then?"

She was shown inside by the Hopkins. Their house was exactly what you would expect from a typical old couple. It was neat and tidy with the kind of colorful wallpaper that was floral or striped.

The living room was nice, a sky blue theme decorated with photos of their children and grandchildren and books and trinkets lining the walls. The kitchen had many pots and pans and other cooking utensils. They had a pleasant dining room with display shelves of dishware and a table laid with a tablecloth that had a bowl of fake fruit sitting on it. Seymour found out it was fake when he tried to take one of the apples, but Cosette was the only one who noticed and couldn't help but laugh to herself.

There were only two bedrooms that were florally decorated by Mrs. Hopkins, and one corner of the main bedroom belonged to Mr. Hopkins' pipe collection.

In short, the house hardly seemed like a place in which a

killer had once resided...at least not anymore.

But every place has its past, and with that past, an imprint of it. Cosette knew that.

"Do you have an attic or a basement?" Cosette asked.

"Why, yes, we have an attic," Mrs. Hopkins replied.

"Smells terrible, but we've got one," Mr. Hopkins added.

"Oh, hush," his wife chided him. "We'll take you to it, dear."

They took her to the attic, and Mr. Hopkins pulled down the ladder.

Mr. Hopkins was right. The attic did smell strange. Like rotting eggs or sour milk, but only faintly. It was filled with the typical things: boxes of Christmas decorations, old furniture and hat boxes, a few old suitcases, and an unused mattress. There was even an old rocking horse that seemed to have been handmade by Mr. Hopkins for his children before they were grown.

"Find anything?" Agent Abberline asked, climbing up the ladder.

"Leave me alone," Cosette replied.

"Oh, okay. Sorry about that," the director answered.

"Are you really going to let her talk to you like that?" Det. Creed asked Abberline in an undertone when he came down.

The director shrugged.

Cosette couldn't see anything out of place. Nothing that showed any signs of a killer having ever lived there. But things aren't always as they seem. She began to inspect the furniture, scrutinizing the bookshelf and the books on it for any signs that something might be concealed inside the spines or pages. She began to tap on the walls and floors, looking especially closely at the discolored places on the walls and floor, and she noticed one strange stain that ran from one place in the middle of the wall down to the floor. It was peculiar for the stain to be where it was, so Cosette touched it and found that it was damp and even a little soft, as if water had been dripping onto it for a while. Grimacing she sanitized her hands with a carry-along hand sanitizer bottle from her bag.

"Does anyone here have a crowbar?" Cosette called down the ladder when she was done.

"I do," Creed replied nonchalantly. "Det. Knox, go fetch it from the car. It's in the trunk."

As he tossed his keys to the rookie detective his keys, the others turned to give the head-detective a bewildered look.

"What?" Creed asked.

"You have a crowbar in the back of your car?" Det. Everglow asked.

"Don't you?" the man replied nonchalantly.

Seymour returned with the crowbar and passed it up to Cosette.

"Oh, and...um...you don't mind if I remove some rotting wood up here, do you?" Cosette asked the Hopkins.

"Oh, I suppose not, dear," Mrs. Hopkins replied.

"We were going to renovate anyways," Mr. Hopkins added.

The girl took the crowbar and began to rip the slabs of wood from the wall until she found what was underneath.

"I found something," Cosette called down to them.

The three detectives, the chief, and the director came up the ladder to see her discovery.

"A freezer in the wall?" Det. Knox asked.

"Welcome to the show, Captain Obvious," Det. Creed said.

Cosette reached over and opened the door of the mini freezer. Water immediately began to spill out onto the floor.

"Oh, God, that smells horrible!" Det. Everglow said, covering her mouth and nose, grimacing at the smell that wafted from the freezer the second the door had been opened.

Cosette noticed a package sitting in the bottom of the freezer. The girl reached in and pulled it out with her pointer finger and thumb before she gave a yelp and tossed the hidden contents in surprise. Creed bent down and picked it up. It was some sort of evidence bag containing at least ten human fingers wrapped in cellophane, some of them even had rings still on them.

"What do you wanna bet these are the fingers of Crane's

victims?" Det. Creed asked, holding the bag up for the others to see.

"So that's what he does with the fingers," Det. Everglow said. "He's keeping them as souvenirs."

"But why would he leave them here?" the chief asked.

"How old would you estimate these are just by looking at them?" Cosette asked Det. Creed.

"Probably as old as his first murder," Creed speculated.

"When did you rent this house?" Cosette asked the Hopkins.

"Oh, only about two years ago," Mrs. Hopkins replied.

"Why would he forget to remove these from the wall though?" Det. Everglow asked.

"Maybe he wanted them found," Cosette suggested. "Maybe he wanted people to know that all these women had been murdered by a singular killer. It was some form of self-accusation."

"So what do you think his next move is going to be?" Chief Abberline asked.

"Same thing it's always been. Blonde, blue-eyed, mid-twenties," Cosette replied.

"Yeah, we know that bit. But we can't put an escort on every damn blonde girl in Virginia."

"I'm not psychic. I can't predict the future by visions; I can only predict by pattern and design," Cosette returned sharply. "All I know is that he's going to go after another woman—another woman like—Det. Everglow."

All eyes suddenly turned to Det. Everglow as everyone had the same idea.

❀❀❀

Agent Abberline promised the Hopkins that the government would pay to have their attic restored before they returned to the station.

Cosette went off with the coroner, Ebenezer Mortensen, to watch him start on the DNA testing while the Abberlines held a conference with Creed and Everglow in the chief's office.

"As we know, Crane is going after particular women, all who look like Nora Crane," the chief said. "We know that Crane is a maniac who kills to escape his problems, not unlike a drug addiction. So how do we catch a drug addict?"

"We lure him in with the drug," Agent Abberline remarked.

"Exactly. When Cosette said what she said yesterday, I saw the pattern from a new angle; one that could benefit us," the chief continued.

"We know who Crane goes after, and we know why. I want to bait him."

Det. Creed and Agent Abberline look to Det. Everglow.

"No, absolutely not," Det. Creed said. "We're not using Eleanor as bait."

"Nothing will happen, Alastor. We'll put her face in the paper, say she's heading the Ripper investigation. We'll give her an escort, body guards, the Crane will take the bait, and we'll catch him, no harm done."

"I said no," Det. Creed barked.

"Why?" Det. Everglow returned suddenly.

"Because it's dangerous," Creed replied.

"Well, you never seemed to care much about that before. You barely talk to me. Frankly, I don't even think you acknowledge me as your partner," Everglow snapped.

"The last time we decided to use someone as bait, they *died.*"

"Alastor, he volunteered to catch the Roadside Reaper," the chief said.

"And you said he wouldn't die, but he did! Angelo was the closest thing I ever had to a brother, and you killed him!"

"The Roadside Reaper killed him," the chief corrected.

"Oh, yeah, I forgot, the Roadside Reaper allowed Angelo to call me while he tore my partner limb from limb with his bare hands and a hunting knife!"

The room went strangely quiet. There was a knock on the door, and Cosette and Mortensen entered just as Det. Creed turned and stormed out, brushing past the girl and nearly knocking her to the floor.

"Great news!" Mortensen announced. "All those fingers match the victims of the Crane. And they were definitely in that freezer for a long time to get that lovely color."

"What was wrong with Creed?" Cosette asked Everglow.

"Abberline wanted to use me as bait for the Crane," Det. Everglow remarked. "He doesn't want me to because of a situation with his old partner."

"What do you want to do, Detective? This is your choice after all," the chief said.

"I want to catch Crane," Everglow replied.

"So you'll act as bait?" the director asked.

"Yes," Everglow said.

Cosette was just leaving when she saw Det. Creed sitting on the bottom step of the station, smoking a cigarette.

"Smoking isn't good for you," she remarked, approaching him and scraping at some weeds growing in the concrete stairs with the toe of her shoe.

"I don't want to hear your goddamn opinion," Det. Creed grunted, flicking the ashes off his cigarette.

"Tell me why you don't want Det. Everglow to be bait for the Crane," Cosette said, sitting down beside the detective.

"I'm not telling you—of all people," Creed returned.

Cosette sighed.

"You and your old partner were close," the girl remarked. "And he's dead now."

"Wow, you're really good with this whole 'comforting' thing," the detective chuckled darkly.

"It's not meant to be comforting; it's meant to be an observation," the girl replied.

Creed rolled his eyes and took a drag of his cigarette. There was a pause between the two of them before she continued: "You have the same amount of guilt as the Crane. How did your partner die? And don't say 'I don't want to talk about it.' I'm already doing 'the Thing.'"

"Then stop doing 'the Thing,'" Creed replied, exhaling the smoke in his lungs.

"You witnessed his death, didn't you?"

"Sort of."

"How so?"

"Over the phone."

"How did he die?"

"Ever heard of the Roadside Reaper?"

"Roadside Reaper—Yeah, Billy Clyde, used to pick up hitchhikers and would mutilate them and kill them—He killed your partner when your partner went after him," Cosette realized.

"And I killed that son of a bitch," Det. Creed said. "I've never driven so fast in my life. As soon as he called me, I was on my way. I got there in time to see his car drive away with my dead partner inside. I followed him back to his cabin, and I shot him with every round I had."

"It's not your fault."

"I didn't stop Angelo from volunteering as bait. I'd call that my fault."

"Someone else would have died in his place. He was a hero."

"I could've saved him."

"Could've, would've, didn't."

"You're about as helpful as cancer," Det. Creed growled.

"You should stop blaming yourself for something you couldn't control."

"Ironic coming from someone who can't get over the fact that she stabbed a serial killer."

"Who told you about that?"

"Abberline."

"Which one?"

"FBI."

"I'll kill him," she muttered.

"I could arrest you for threatening the director's life," he smirked.

"You wouldn't do that."

Det. Creed hummed, dragging on his cigarette.

"Look, I'm not asking you to get over it. I'm telling you it's not your fault," Cosette remarked. "Det. Everglow has decided she's going to put herself out as bait for Crane and that's whether you like it or not. Now, you can either wallow in your regret or catch the Crane like the head-detective that you are."

"My partner's name was Angelo Emrys by the way."

"Angelo Emrys... ," Cosette said.

"You know, I don't know why I'm telling you any of this."

"Because I'm easy to talk to."

"And you've got that creepy psychic thing."

"That's true. I still don't like you though. You're a grumpy old man," Cosette said, plucking the cigarette from his hands and stomping it out.

"Yeah, well, the feeling's mutual, brat," Det. Creed sighed, shaking his head.

Chapter Seventeen:

Cosette was up early the next morning to head down to the police station. When she reached the station, she went straight to Chief Abberline's office where she found—

"Pandora?" What are you doing here?" Cosette asked, stopping in her tracks upon seeing the reporter and her cameraman in the station.

"Oh, hello, sweetheart. I suppose no one told you then," Pandora Crestmont said condescendingly.

"Abberline, I thought I would be doing the report on Det. Everglow," Cosette said, whirling around to face the director, who stood behind his wife's chair.

"Ah, no, Cosette. You write short stories and novels, not newspaper reports. If you were to do it, it would be a conflict of interest," Abberline replied.

"You're really going to trust this lying Dalilah? You couldn't have at least found someone better?"

"We thought that because Ms. Crestmont has already written so much on the Crane, it wouldn't be surprising for her to have another article," the director remarked.

"In other words, we won't be needing you, sweetie, so run along," Pandora sang caustically. "Conrad, come along. We have to get pictures for the article."

"Hang on, I want to sit in on the interview. After all, I'm

pretty sure I can tell you what to say that will piss off the Crane," Cosette remarked.

"Oh, I don't think so, honey—" Ms. Crestmont began.

"Of course, Cosette," Chief Abberline said, frowning at Pandora. "We would love your help."

Pandora glared at Cosette as they made their way to the conference room. The reporter sat down across from the two detectives, and Cosette sauntered, listening and examining the things that sat around the room. Conrad began to snap pictures, and Pandora clicked on her voice recorder, setting it down on the table in front of her and folding her hands in front of her.

"So, Det. Everglow, you are heading the investigation of the Crane?" Pandora asked.

"Don't call him the Crane," Cosette interjected. "Call him the Virginia Copycat. He surely won't appreciate Mr. Herrod getting the credit for his methods."

Pandora raised an eyebrow, but nodded.

"Alright, are you heading the Copycat case?"

"Yes, I am," Det. Everglow said. "It is truly a great privilege for me to lead this case, especially as new as I am. But I definitely wouldn't be here without my partner—"

"What do you think the public should know about the Copycat?" Pandora interrupted. "What are things that they should be wary of?"

"Well, I think the first thing people should know is that the Virginia Copycat goes after young women with blonde hair and blue eyes. We suspect this is because they have exceptional resemblance to—"

"The women he's sexually attracted to," Cosette interrupted, all heads turned to her.

"What, Cosette?" Det. Everglow asked in surprise.

"Just put it in," the girl said. "He is in every way a perverted maniac."

"Okay...His main drive is sex, and he has absolutely no respect for women. He is a bigot. But then he kills his victims to uphold his dignity. No body, no crime in his mind," Everglow said, catching on to Cosette's idea.

"The Copycat is a heartless monster and a sexual deviant, as well as being completely unoriginal, having stolen his murder tactics off a petty killer who murdered his wife in the exact same way."

"And his habit of cutting off their middle finger due to the guilt he feels for killing his very first victim, his own wife."

"This is a sign that he probably cheated on her as well, killing her so that the other woman wouldn't catch him," Cosette added.

"And he should be put behind bars before he can harm anyone else," Det. Everglow finished.

All heads turned towards the door then as Det. Knox burst in.

"Chief, it's the jail!" Seymour exclaimed breathlessly. "It's about Herrod. Line one in your office."

The chief raised her eyebrows and followed Seymour to her office.

"Continue on," Agent Abberline said, and followed his wife.

The others did continue while the chief talked on the phone. She talked with the jail for a while. Cosette could see her from the window of the conference room through the window of her office. She looked concerned, and Cosette wondered what was being said. At last they reentered the conference room.

"We'll have to finish this interview later," Chief Abberline said. "We've got to get down to the jail."

"All of us?" Pandora asked.

"No, you need to start on the article."

"What about me?" Cosette asked.

"I think it would be helpful," Chief Aberline said.

"What happened?" Agent Abberline asked.

"Herrod escaped," the chief remarked.

"What?" the director asked. "That's not good. Especially with the Crane out there."

"My thoughts exactly," the chief agreed.

❀❀❀

They got down to the station as soon as they could and hurried inside. The chief found the security guard who had called her at once, and he updated her on all that had happened.

"The guard said that Herrod escaped last night. He wasn't here, but he said when they day shift got in they found the cell door wide open," Chief Abberline related.

"Look at this," Cosette said, examining the cell door.

"What is it?" the director asked, trying to see what the girl meant. "There isn't anything there."

"Exactly," Cosette said. "If Herrod had picked the lock, he would have used wire or something he could get his hands on and that would leave scratches and scuff marks."

"Maybe he managed to steal the keys off the nightguard?" Det. Everglow suggested.

"Who *were* the nightguards?" Cosette inquired.

"Um...let's see, there was Bobby, David, Darik—"

"Can we see the files of the men on duty last night?" the chief asked.

"Certainly. Let me grab it,"

"Hey, Marty, do you have the new guy's file?"

"Which one, Don?" Marty asked.

"There's only one new guy, Marty."

"Uh...here it is. His name, Darik Heron, started here about a week or two ago. Pretty good guy, and all his paperwork checked out," Marty said, examining the file, and handing it over to the chief to look at for herself.

"Can we get a copy of this file?" Chief Abberline asked.

"Yeah, here, I'll make a copy of it now," Don said, turning to the printer on their desk. "He isn't in any trouble, is he?"

"Probably," the chief replied, taking the copy of the file Don gave her.

Finally, Don took them to the security room to inspect the footage. They quickly found the footage from the night before and checked the camera for the murder. When they reached the supposed time of death, they found that someone had shut off the cameras from the time before the escape and when it turned back on, only five minutes later, Herrod was gone and the cell was wide open.

"Wait a minute, someone shut down the cameras?" the guard asked in confusion.

"Because your associate shut it off," Agent Abberline said.

"Are you saying that Heron murdered that prisoner?" the guard asked.

"Oh for goodness' sakes!" Cosette exclaimed suddenly.

"What?" Creed asked.

"Herons are birds often mistaken for cranes," the girl remarked.

"So—? Oh," the head-detective said in realization. "Draven Crane was the security guard."

"Do you have any photographs of him?" Det. Everglow asked the security guard.

"Yes, here," the guard said, handing a photo to her.

It was a picture of a tan, middle-aged man with brown hair and eyes.

"Hey, I bumped into him the last time I visited Herrod," Cosette remarked.

"He looks nothing like Crane, though," Det. Everglow stated.

"He probably disguised himself," Chief Abberline said.

"Well, we've got an address from the file," Agent Abberline said, looking up from the file. "What do you say we try to nail this guy now?"

❀❀❀

They all drove to the address that was given in Darik Heron's file. The S.W.A.T team that had been called by Agent Abberline, who was waiting for them upon their arrival. The house was in the middle of a pleasant neighborhood and looked quite similar to Mrs. Crane's and the Hopkins' house.

On Abberline's mark, the S.W.A.T team kicked in the door and flooded inside. Upon entering, they found that the house was vacant except for a couple of boxes. When the door crashed down, someone came running out from one of the bedrooms. It was a young man with fair hair and blue eyes.

"Hey, what's going on here?" the young man shouted.

"Who are you?" Agent Abberline asked, lowering his gun.

"Mark Alfreds," the man said.

"You aren't related to Emma Alfreds by any chance?" Det. Everglow asked.

"Yes, she was my sister."

"Is this your house?" Agent Abberline asked.

"It was. Emma and I shared the rent. I'm actually just about to leave. I can't afford it alone along with my tuition. Why are you here?" Mark asked.

"We're investigating your sister's murder," Agent Abberline said.

"Oh, so, why are you here then—I mean, why are you here with a S.W.A.T team?"

"Our apologies. We thought this was the house of the Richmond Ripper. He signed something with this same address. Perhaps you could tell us who is renting the house now?"

"Yeah, some old lady named Aggie Perkins, I think," Mark replied. "Why would he use our address?"

"So we wouldn't find him," the director replied.

"Everything he's done is a clue," Cosette said. "He's probably laughing at us right now."

"Who are you?" Mark asked, noticing the girl for the first time.

"I'm Cosette," Cosette clarified.

"Oh."

Agent Abberline rang Seymour and asked him to check up on Mrs. Perkins and make certain she wasn't just another one of the Crane's aliases. When it checked out, Abberline called off the S.W.A.T team.

"We're sorry for startling you like this, Mr. Alfreds," Agent Abberline said. "We know you've been through so much already."

"Hey, as long as you catch the bastard who killed my sister," Mark replied.

❀❀❀

Cosette returned to her apartment, thinking only of sleep and the Klondike ice cream bar in her freezer. Just as she unlocked her door and went into her apartment, she stumbled over something on the threshold. She looked down to see the tupperware she had lent the neighbor.

Picking it up, she found that it was full of some sort of colorful paper. She took it inside, shutting the door behind her. Magnolia hopped up on the counter as Cosette opened the tupperware and dumped its contents onto the countertop. It turned out to be a bunch of origami birds. Cosette enjoyed origami and recognized the folded birds at once. They were paper cranes. There was a note as well. It read:

Dear Cosette,

Thank you so much for my housewarming gift. I enjoyed them so much. You are so kind.

Truly,

Your Neighbor.

Cosette stared at the note in concern. She hadn't given her name to her neighbor. How had this person discovered it? Still, perhaps the neighbor had simply asked Jimmy for her name, and he just happened to know how to fold paper birds. She thought that it would still be worth mentioning to Agent Abberline.

She went to pick up her phone, but when she opened it, she found that she had gotten an email. It was the published article on Det. Everglow sent from Pandora Crestmont. It read:

Hunting the Copycat: Unveiling a Monster in Virginia

By Pandora Crestmont

Photography By Conrad Finnigan

The Virginia Copycat has been rampaging through the country for ten years now, bringing tragedy and despair wherever he goes.

I sat for an interview with the chief of local police, Carol Abberline, as well as the Behavioral Analysis Unit's director, Arnold Abberline, and Det. Eleanor Everglow, who will be heading this case, and Head-Det. Alastor Creed and Cosette Bordeaux, with the Virginia Times.

They are working as quickly and efficiently as they can to catch the Copycat and have discovered a good amount about this killer.

One prominent trait about the Virginia Copycat is that he is sexually driven in his actions, most always towards blonde, blue-eyed young women.

"He's a perverted maniac driven completely by sex," says Det. Everglow. "He is a sexist bigot with absolutely no respect for women. He kills them in order to uphold their dignity, because in his mind, no body equals no crime."

Ultimately, the Virginia Copycat is a heartless monster and a sexual deviant, slitting his victims' throats and cutting off their middle finger due to the guilt he feels for killing his very first victim, his own wife, most likely due to alleged adultery, and, worst of all, he is completely unoriginal, having stolen his murder tactics off Thomas Herrod, who you can read about in my interview titled ***Killer: The Path To Uxoricide****.*

Ultimately, the police want the Virginia Copycat behind bars before he can harm anyone else.

Above was a photograph taken of the Abberlines, Det. Everglow, Det. Creed, and Pandora.

There really wasn't anything wrong with the article except for the fact that both Abberlines had explicitly said not to put Cosette's name on the article at all so as not to put her in any danger.

Cosette searched Pandora up on the internet and found her phone number and immediately called her.

"You put my name on the article!" Cosette exclaimed as soon as the reporter picked up.

"Yes, sweetie, I did, but I also put everyone else's names on it, so what about it?"

"You weren't supposed to! I'm not even really *with* the FBI! You could have just put *me* in serious danger!"

"Oh, please, dear, we're *all* in danger after I published that story."

"Does Abberline know about this?"

"Not unless he read the published edition of the article," Pandora drawled.

"You did this on purpose!" Cosette accused.

"Let's just say that I don't like being insulted," Ms. Crestmont remarked.

Cosette hung up with a groan, rubbing her eyes wearily before she called Abberline.

"Abberline, have you read Pandora's article yet?"

"Not the published version."

"Whose names were supposed to be mentioned in the article again?"

"Um...Det. Everglow's obviously, Det. Creed, my wife, myself, the article. Why?"

"*Ms. Crestmont* added my name—and admitted to doing it out of spite."

"What?"

"Well, it's clear that she doesn't *like* me."

"Damnit," Abberline growled. "I'm not sure we have enough time to remove it. I can still see if she can, but the Crane may have already seen it."

"Yeah, I know, it's alright. I guess either way, one of us will attract the Crane."

Chapter Eighteen:

Cosette had been utterly irritated by Pandora's article. Agent Abberline had attempted to pull it but he later called her and informed her that the story had been circulating too long for them to fix it now.

She spent the rest of the day typing up the new novel with Magnolia sitting on the desk and swatting at the computer keys as the girl typed. She finally moved from the desk to the couch after making herself a butter and cucumber sandwich with a slice of cheddar cheese, and a Lindor white chocolate for a late lunch.

The girl had nearly finished converting the instances in her notebook onto the computer when she became enthralled with the show playing on television in the background, despite having seen that episode eight times give or take.

She was rather zoned out, her hands positioned to type on the keyboard, but not moving, and startled when she heard something hit the bedroom window.

Curious as to what it had been, she got up and went to the bedroom, followed by the cat. She looked out without sliding the window open. It hadn't sounded large enough to be a bird, but she didn't see anything outside. She had just returned to the couch when she heard something hit the window again and rushed to it once more, throwing the window open and looking down.

There she saw a figure standing, barely visible, in the alley below. Cosette could make the figure out, though, as Thomas Herrod.

They stared at each other momentarily, Cosette wide-eyed and in surprise, Herrod impatiently; then he turned and hurried into the darkness.

"Wait!" Cosette called.

She climbed out the window and let down the fire escape.

"Watch the apartment for me while I'm gone," the girl told her cat as she closed the window.

She rushed down the fire escape and dropped to the ground. As soon as she did, she noticed something on the ground, waiting for her. It was a stone wrapped in paper. She picked up the rock and took the paper off, turning it over. It read:

Meet me at Southern States Silo midnight tonight.

Curiouser and curiouser.

-T. H

Cosette looked around one last time to see if Herrod had really disappeared. When she was sure he wasn't around, she climbed back up the fire escape and through her window, back into her apartment and contemplated the note.

Of course she was going to meet Herrod, and of course she wasn't going to call the police.

So at midnight that night she grabbed her purse, checked to make certain she had her knife and pepper spray, as well as her phone and notebook and left through the fire escape again and made her way on foot to the old warehouse. The Southern State Silo was a tall, aged cylindrical towers made of concrete. They were rusted and covered in graffiti and overgrown vegetation. It was rather eerie on the outside, especially in the dark. Cosette couldn't wait to see the inside.

She walked around the building a little to see if there were any signs of Herrod being there. It didn't seem as if anyone had been around for quite a while, so she went up to the front doors and pulled on them. She found that they were in fact open and went inside.

It was a rather spacious interior with concrete walls and floors made to support heavy loads, though now they were broken and grimy. The place was dimly lit and there were remnants of old machinery, scrap metal, and graffiti on the dirty walls.

She walked around the place, the heels of her shoes tapping quietly on the floor. A thrill ran down her spine at the idea of being in such a mysterious place.

"Cosette!"

She spun around, clutching her bag, which she had nearly dropped in surprise, to see Thomas Herrod come out from behind a stack of old crates.

"Mr. Herrod," Cosette remarked.

"Part of me didn't think you would be coming at all," Herrod chuckled.

"Of course I'm here. The story isn't complete without the answers. So tell me," Cosette prompted, putting one hand into the singular pocket on the front of her skirt.

"How much did the Crane woman tell you?"

"She told us everything about Crane's childhood, how he met Nora, how she helped him fake his death, and how she found the finger in her backyard and eventually spoke with you. She also mentioned a little about what had happened the night Amanda was murdered."

"Good, then you know most of it. Now let me tell you exactly what happened the night my wife was murdered," Herrod said, sitting down on a crate and Cosette followed suit. "Amanda was the best thing that ever happened to me." He paused to look for Cosette's reaction. "Cheesy right? But not everyone gets the best childhood. I had an alcoholic father, but I still knew my parents loved me. In fact, I had a decent relationship with them before I was arrested. Amanda and I didn't have much—she was a secretary at the bank, and I was an accountant. That's how we met.

"After we had gotten married, though, Amanda began to

notice that one customer would stare at her every time he would come to the bank. She always felt like she was being followed when she went out alone, but, at the end of the day, we both dismissed it. After a while, the man asked her out, but of course she told him she was married. After that, he stopped coming to the bank, though Amanda had actually noticed a figure following her around.

"One night, I went to Amanda's favorite Greek restaurant and stopped by the store to get her some flowers and chocolate for our date night, but when I got back, she was lying in the middle of the living room, murdered, and I had caught that bastard in the act of cutting off her finger. As soon as he saw me, he leaped up and tackled me before I could get out. I tried to fight him off, but he overpowered me and tried to kill me.

"I shamefully begged him not to. I told him that if he let me live I wouldn't tell anyone what I had seen. I promised him that I would take the fall for the murder, and he would remain unknown. He thought about this and finally agreed to it, but he said that if I told anyone, he would kill me, and to prove his seriousness, he stabbed me. You know the rest."

Cosette nodded.

"May I ask why you decided to tell me all this?"

"You believe me more than anyone else. You're different. You radiate a kindness and empathy...like...it made me feel like I could talk to you," he paused to recollect himself. "But, as I'm sure you've realized, I didn't escape from jail. I was let out. Crane was the new security guard on duty. He had read all of that Crestmont woman's articles, and he knew I was going to tell everyone. The thing is, he's fair. He let me out and told me that I could try to escape, but he'd catch me eventually. I know it's only a matter of time before I die," Herrod said, shaking his head with a smile.

"You don't have to. If you come back to the police station with me, they could protect you until we catch Crane," the girl remarked.

"No," Herrod said. "I think...I think I want to die facing Crane. If he catches me, I want to die exactly how I deserved to ten years ago."

Cosette frowned sympathetically.

"I don't know why I did what I did: lying to stay alive. I'm a coward. Everyone thinks I killed the person I love most in this world. I'm just tired of it. I'd like to say I did it with the hope that I could somehow stop Crane, but I think seeing what he had done to Amanda made me afraid to die. I'm *tired* of being a coward. I'm not going to play his games. I'm not going to hide from him anymore. This is my guilt, this is my grief, it's time for me to face it."

"So I can't convince you to come back with me?" the girl asked, a hint of sorrow in her tone.

"No," the man replied, standing up. "Just tell them everything I told you."

The conversation was clearly over. Cosette remained sitting on the crate as Herrod made his way towards the warehouse doors.

"Oh, and Cosette," he said.

"Yes?"

"Tell them to bury me beside my wife."

"I will," Cosette promised.

"Goodbye, Cosette. Thank you for everything," Thomas Herrod said.

With that, the man went out. The girl waited until she heard the sound of a car, which must have been hidden somewhere, as she hadn't seen it when she looked around. Then she stood and sighed. Taking her phone out of her pocket, she pressed the save button on her recorder.

"Goodbye, Mr. Herrod," she said.

Chapter Nineteen:

Cosette brought the recording she had taken of an unsuspecting Herrod straight to the chief of police.

The woman listened to it with raised eyebrows, and when it was over, she sighed, folding her hands on the desk.

"So, Herrod decided he wanted to be bait," Chief Abberline said.

"He knows he's going to die," Cosette remarked. "He wants the Crane to catch him. "He *wants* to die."

The chief nodded.

"But the sacrifice he intends to make could lead us closer to Crane. Besides, now that we have Herrod telling his story, we'll have more evidence against Crane in court. Although I wish you had called someone to accompany you."

"He asked me to come alone."

"Yes, but what if the Crane had followed him. That wouldn't have ended well," the chief said. "Next time, call one of us, and we'll come to back you up."

"Do you think there will be a next time?" Cosette asked the woman. "For me, I mean."

"I think you have a knack for getting yourself into trouble," the chief replied.

Chapter Twenty:

"Have you ever wanted to die?" Cosette asked, standing in Dr. Carnifex's office, staring at the butterflies hanging on the walls.

"Not particularly," the doctor replied. "Have you?"

"Yes," the girl replied. "But I'm not asking for myself. Mr. Herrod met with me the other night and told me everything."

"Oh, and what brought about his change of mind to be more cooperative?"

"He said that he felt guilty for living when Amanda had died. He said he was tired of being a coward."

"Would you say his survival was cowardice?" the doctor asked.

"No," Cosette replied. "I don't think he's a coward either way."

"But he does," Dr. Carnifex said understandingly.

"He thinks by facing the Crane he'll be facing—oh, how did he put it? He said it was his guilt and his grief and by facing the Crane, he would be facing all of that."

"What do you think about it?"

"I don't want to think he's right because that would mean he should have died all that time ago."

"Perhaps his death would have broken Crane's pattern, though it would have led the police to the same conclusions that you have all come to now. Herrod dying then would have been more of a cowardice than him living. What I mean to say is that sometimes, you have to face your problems—that guilt and that grief, or you'll become something much like the Crane."

"But I already killed Sanguini," Cosette said, frowning.

"Perhaps the Northeast Nightmare is not the thing that you needed to face. Perhaps you need to face yourself," Dr. Carnifex said.

"Myself?" the girl repeated. "How do I do that?"

"I don't know. Sometimes there are things you have to make sense of on your own."

"Well, a lot of help you are," Cosette grumbled.

❀❀❀

It was Sunday. Det. Knox called the chief early that morning before the sun had even risen. He sounded frantic when he told her the news.

"They found Herrod!" the junior detective exclaimed.

"Where?" the chief asked.

"He's back in his cell."

"Alive?"

"No, he's definitely dead. They said they found him as soon as they got in this morning."

"Well, we knew this was going to happen," the chief sighed.

"Hey, what's going on? It's 6 A.M," Agent Abberline whispered, rolling over to see what his wife was doing.

"Herrod's dead," his wife answered grimly.

"What! So soon?"

"Seymour, can you call Det. Creed, Det. Everglow and Dr. Vale and tell them to meet us at the station?"

"Yes, at once, ma'am," Seymour answered.

When the chief had gotten off the phone she got out of bed and went to get ready to go down to the station. Abberline got up as well.

"We need to call Cosette and inform her what has happened," Abberline said.

"No," the chief replied at once.

"Why not?"

"I don't think it would be helpful for *her*," Chief Abberline replied.

"It could be helpful for *us*. Besides, she's the only one who could get any information from him. I think she deserves to come along."

The chief sighed.

"Alright, fine, whatever. You're higher up in government rank than me anyways," his wife remarked disapprovingly as she grabbed her coat.

❀❀❀

Cosette had gone to the early Mass at the local parish as she always did. She was right outside her apartment when her phone began to ring. She saw that it was Agent Abberline and picked up at once.

"Cosette, you ought to come down to the station at once."

"Why, what happened?" the girl asked.

"It's Herrod."

"Is Mr. Herrod—?"

"Yes."

"Oh," Cosette remarked. "Well, I suppose it was to be expected. I'll be over right away."

She turned round and all but flew to the police station.

When she arrived, Abberline was waiting out front with his car for her.

"Everyone else has gone ahead," the director remarked.

"Well, let's not waste time," Cosette replied. "I'm sure they've already set up the crime scene."

Dr. Vale was waiting for them outside the jail when they arrived.

"How far did they get in setting up the crime scene?" Agent Abberline asked her.

"They're nearly done," Dr. Vale replied.

Agent Abberline continued into the jail, but Dr. Vale stopped Cosette.

"Carol asked me to talk to you before you went in," the doctor said.

"Why?"

"She wanted to make sure you were alright before you saw all of it. It really is rather disturbing. And she said you and Herrod were friends."

"We weren't 'friends,'" Cosette replied. 'He just had information I needed. Seeing as how he gave it to me already, I'd really like to just go inside."

"Cosette, are you sure you're...alright?"

"Define 'alright,'" the girl said.

"You just seem a little different than the last time we really talked together."

"Well, I was seven, had both my parents, and hadn't murdered a serial killer, so I would dare say I've changed a bit. I think I'd be more concerned if I had stayed the same."

Dr. Vale frowned slightly but didn't say anything more.

Cosette went into the jail followed by Dr. Vale and found quite a macabre spectacle waiting inside for her.

Thomas Herrod hung, lifeless, from the ceiling of his cell, though this seemed rather redundant as his throat had already been cut, staining the rope around his neck a deep crimson. The whole jail cell was splattered with blood and smelled like sickly sweet death. Cosette noticed that both Herrod's ring fingers had also been removed.

"He was killed by the Crane," Det. Creed remarked.

"Obviously," the chief returned. "My question is, why would the Crane bring him back to his cell after releasing him from it? And how was he able to get past security? I specifically had them keep an eye out for Crane."

"Crane brought Mr. Herrod's corpse back to his cell for aesthetic purposes," Cosette remarked, inspecting the cell and the body hanging inside. "He's letting us all know that he won his little game. At least, in his mind. In reality, Herrod wins seeing as how this is exactly what he wanted to happen. As for how he got past security, though, I'm not sure."

"I've already asked for cameras to be pulled," Det. Everglow remarked.

"Good idea," the chief said. "Don, we need to use the surveillance room again."

"Absolutely," Don replied.

They went through the last night's security footage and half expected the film to have been cut off when Crane strung Herrod up in his cell, but as it turned out, the video showed Crane, disguised as Heron, hanging up the body.

"How did he get in?" Det. Creed exclaimed. "Are these guys really that stupid?"

"We're not stupid, we were just switching shifts," Don replied offendedly.

"Why would Crane not cut the security cameras again?" Det. Everglow asked.

"Maybe he wanted us to know he killed Herrod," Dr. Vale suggested.

"He's angry," Cosette agreed. "He wants to let us know that we've angered him."

"Maybe this all has to do with the article," Dr. Vale said.

"That's how he found out Herrod was telling on him," Det. Everglow said.

"But we still have no idea where this guy even is," Det. Creed remarked.

"Let's finish investigating the crime scene. Maybe that will yield something," Abberline suggested.

❀❀❀

Cosette stood in front of Herrod's bloody cell.

Agent Abberline had called for the morticians to come and take the corpse, but he hadn't arrived yet. So she stared at the bloody body hanging from the ceiling. Herrod's eyes were wide open, staring, unblinkingly back at her.

Then he lifted his head.

"Hello, Miss Bordeaux. I know we both expected this would happen."

Cosette stared at the corpse in momentary shock before

she gave a sigh.

"Yes, we did."

"But I'm dead now," Herrod sighed.

Cosette nodded.

"Do you feel as though you have faced your cowardice?" Cosette asked.

"Yes," Herrod croaked. "Thank you. But have you faced *your* cowardice?"

"No," Cosette replied plainly.

"You should."

"How?"

"That's something only you can figure out."

"Well, that isn't much help at all then."

"Have you remembered to tell them to bury me beside my wife?"

"I was going to wait to tell them until you were dead in hopes you survived."

"Well, make sure you tell them."

"I will," Cosette promised.

"Cosette..."

❀❀❀

"Cosette!"

"Cosette jolted out of her stupor to find that Det. Everglow was shaking her. The girl hurriedly checked to make certain that Herrod's corpse was quite dead.

"We're going to the address Crane gave. Do you want to come along?"

"Yes," Cosette answered. "And we must remember to bury Mr. Herrod beside his wife."

❀❀❀

Cosette had been left alone in the morgue with the corpse of Thomas Herrod.

The others had gone off to discuss the murder, but she couldn't bring herself to peel her eyes away from his dead, open eyes staring up and reflecting the fluorescent lighting.

She noticed that the man's throat looked strange, almost

as if something was inside it. Curious, she picked up the scalpel sitting on the metal tray beside her and without fully knowing what she was doing she cut Herrod's crusted throat open again.

Red blood spilled out over her hands, surprisingly warm for that of a corpse. It was nauseating and somehow comforting. She flexed her fingers as the blood dripped off of them, staining them red.

Just then, something inside the open gash began to move. Cosette watched in a daze as a butterfly flew out and landed on her hands. Another butterfly and another butterfly flew out of the corpse's throat, surrounding Cosette until they seemed to blanket her.

Then she caught a glimpse of herself in the mortuary body tray doors.

Drenched in blood and staring back at her with those cold, empty eyes the butterflies alighting from her flower crown... surely this couldn't be her own reflection.

"Who are you?"

"Wh-what?" Cosette asked.

"Who are you?"

"I don't know what you mean."

"Who *are* you?" the thing pressed.

It lifted its hands up to push on the silver doors, and to the girl's shock, they began to crack like the glass of a mirror. Cosette began to back away.

"*Who are you*?"

"I'm Cosette Bordeaux," Cosette replied, back farther away still.

"*Who are you*?"

"I said I'm Cosette Bordeaux!" the girl exclaimed, her back hitting the wall behind her.

Though despite being across the room, the reflection seemed to be right up pressing upon her.

"Who are you!"

"I don't know!" Cosette shouted.

And she struck at the mirror with all her might, the shards

bursting under her fingers, the reflection shattering into a million pieces, though she could still hear the haunting question ringing in her ears.

Chapter Twenty-One:

Cosette woke with a start, breathing hard. She caught her breath as she looked groggily around, trying to figure out where she was. Looking around she found that she was in her room. Magnolia was sitting upright on the end of her bed, staring at her in irritation at being so suddenly woken. She felt a sudden breeze on her face and realized that her window was open, though she was certain she hadn't unlocked or opened it. Slipping out of bed, she went to close it and drew the curtains, frowning.

She realized that she was trembling and decided to make a cup of hot chocolate for herself to try to calm down. Cosette went into the living room and cut the television on, making her way across to the kitchen and grabbing the kettle by its light. She turned towards the sink to fill the kettle with water when she stopped dead in her tracks at the site of a brown cardboard box sitting on her counter. The box had certainly not been there before she had gone to bed.

The girl thought of the open window. That, paired with the mysterious appearance of a box in her apartment, could only mean an intruder. She approached the box with caution and inspected it curiously. There was no stamp on it and no address of any sort. The box was in decent condition and must have been hand delivered. She took some scissors from one of the kitchen drawers and cut the tape holding the box closed. Upon opening it, she was met with blue tissue paper. Removing it, she saw what was underneath and gave a gasp of disgust. On top of a pile of colorful paper cranes was a severed finger.

Cosette made a rush for her room, nearly tripping over the cat as she went to fetch her phone. She dialed, and it rang several times before she received an answer.

"Cosette? Are you alright?" Agent Abberline answered blearily.

"Someone just broke into my apartment," Cosette remarked.

"What? Are you alright?"

"Yes, I'm fine; they didn't do anything to me. But they left me a...present."

"What was it?"

"Thomas Herrod's finger."

"It must have been the Crane. Did you check your apartment to make sure he's not still there?" Abberline asked.

"No, I called you."

"Nevermind, just get out of your apartment and go wait in the lobby. I'll be down there in just a few minutes. Just stay on the phone with me until I arrive."

While waiting, Cosette searched the house for any place an intruder could have been hiding, though found no one. The director was quick to arrive followed by Creed and Everglow.

"Cosette, are you alright?" Abberline asked upon arrival.

"Yes, I'm fine," Cosette replied.

"Where is the finger?" Abberline asked.

"Right here," Cosette replied, opening the freezer and pulling the finger out.

"Oh, for the love of God, don't put something dead with your food!" Creed reprimanded as the girl handed the director the box.

"I looked around and didn't find anyone here. Crane must have come just to leave that finger."

"That's fine, but I've already gotten Carol to have her men

search the building for Crane," Abberline remarked. "One thing's for sure, you can't stay here right now. It would be best for you to go with Det. Everglow until we can sort things out."

Cosette decided to be agreeable and left the complex with Everglow and Magnolia, whom she had refused to leave behind. Chief Abberline and several other police cars arrived at the apartment building shortly after they had gone. The chief was stoney faced as the officers checked over the building for any sign of Crane still inside.

"You know what this means, don't you?" she asked her husband.

"But why would Crane want Cosette? She had nothing to do with the article."

"You said Pandora put her name in the story we put out."

"Yes, but that shouldn't have affected anything. How could he have known who she was?"

"He pretended to be a security guard at the jail where Herrod was kept. He could have overheard her talking with him and decided to target her. I mean, she fits the bait."

"This isn't good," the agent muttered.

"No, it's not," his wife agreed.

"What do we do?"

"She needs to be put somewhere safe where Crane won't be able to get to her. Somewhere he won't think to look for her. I think, too, she needs a parental guardian to assist her until she is able—and of age—to live alone," the chief remarked.

"That's a wise idea, though I'm not sure how well Cosette will take it," Abberline said.

"Perhaps she wouldn't be so opposed if she was staying with someone she knew," the chief suggested.

"You're right," the director agreed. "I should contact Vale. She has known Cosette the longest."

Chapter Twenty-Two:

After leaving Cosette's apartment, Det. Everglow had taken them to a Waffle House where they had sat for nearly an hour and a half, though Cosette seemed nervous and unsettled, hardly eating anything. Everglow supposed anyone would be disconcerted knowing a murderer snuck in while she was sleeping and then finding a dead body part in her house. They didn't have too long to wait before Creed called his partner, and she excused herself a short distance from the table.

"Hey, did they find anything?" Everglow asked.

"No, he wasn't here. Abberline wants you to bring the kid back to the complex to pack her bags."

"Pack her bags?"

"Yeah, he says it's not safe for her to stay in her apartment alone anymore, so they're sending her to stay with someone," Creed replied. "But he said not to tell her anything. They'll explain it to her when she gets here."

"She's not going to like this," Everglow said.

"Well, she'll cooperate if she doesn't want Crane to come after her."

"Is he after her?" Everglow asked.

"We can't be certain."

Everglow sighed.

"Alright, I'll bring her back."

When the detective and the girl arrived, the police were getting ready to take the finger in for testing. Abberline opened his mouth to explain the situation to Cosette, but she interrupted him before he could say anything, distracted by the man from forensics who had come to retrieve the finger.

"Has Thomas Herrod had his autopsy yet?" she asked abruptly.

Agent Abberline paused before he replied, "Not yet, but Edgar just came to pick up the finger that you found in your apartment. I suspect they'll go ahead and get an early start on the autopsy."

"Then we have to go at once. I want to be there to make sure of something," Cosette said.

"I don't think that's a good idea—"

"You don't understand. I think I figured something out about Herrod's murder, and I have to be there to make sure of it."

Agent Abberline was against the idea of Cosette accompanying them to the autopsy and tried to persuade her otherwise, but she determinedly insisted. And "insisted" meaning that she told him exactly how she would break into the morgue to see Thomas Herrod's body if she wasn't allowed to accompany.

When they reached the morgue, Mortensen wasn't working alone. Cosette had only seen him work once, and he had been by himself. This time around he had help from two men with blond hair, one darker than the other, and a woman with very long blonde hair that had been dyed pink at the tips and braided. They all had the same gray eyes.

"Oh, hello, Cosette," Mortensen said when she entered after the Abberlines and the two detectives. "Glad to see you again. Have you met the rest of the family?"

"Um...I don't think so," Cosette said.

"Well, these are my sons, Edgar and Allan," Mortensen said.

"Greetings," said Edgar, who was older.

"And salutations," Allan, who was younger, said.

Edgar looked to be only in his late thirties, and his hair was nearly completely gray though his face looked young and serious. Allan was only a little younger than Edgar by the looks of things, with blond hair and a sharp face that was particularly cheerful for someone who worked in a morgue.

"I've never actually met two people named Edgar and Allan. I thought that was only in the movies. I really love that," Cosette remarked. "You know, I'm actually related to Edgar Allan Poe."

"Really?" Edgar asked.

"Yes. He's a cousin by marriage."

"That's very interesting," Allan remarked.

"And let me guess," Cosette said to the woman. "You must be Poe."

"No," the woman remarked. "I'm Ladybug."

"Ladybug?" Cosette asked.

"Yes. Like the insect."

"Did you know that you can't actually tell a ladybug's age by the number of its spots? They're just a species-specific trait."

"I did," Ladybug said. "They're very interesting creatures really. Did you know that they will secrete a foul tasting liquid all over their legs to deter predators?"

"Yes, I knew that as well. You know, it's so nice to meet someone with an insect name. My middle name is Helenor, like the morpho blue helenor butterfly."

"No way, that's fascinating," Ladybug returned with a grin.

"Can we get back on track?" Creed snapped.

"Oh, yes, of course," Ladybug said.

"So what about the autopsy?" Det. Creed asked.

"Well, we didn't find any fingerprints or useful DNA on the body," Edgar remarked.

"And I think the cause of death is pretty obvious," Allan said.

"He was perfectly healthy, no organ or heart failure, and no signs of poison or anything. He just got his throat slit, both his ring fingers cut off, and then he was strung up," Ladybug said.

"Yes, that bit was for the theatrics, wasn't it?" Mortensen agreed. "He did try to put up a fight, though, discerning from those subcutaneous bruises all over he body, several lacerations and abrasions caused by a knife and fingernails. And that one finger that was gifted to you, Cosette, is definitely his."

"My question is, where did the other finger go," Edgar wondered aloud.

"Taking both doesn't quite fit his pattern," Allan agreed.

"Have you checked inside his throat yet?" Cosette asked.

"Why, no, we haven't yet," Mortensen said.

"Can you?"

"Of course. How very *Silence of the Lambs*."

Mortensen took up his scalpel and expertly sliced through the dried blood, which had crusted his throat back together. He then took some tweezers, which Ladybug handed him, and poked around in the wound.

"Hold on a minute," Mortensen said, taking up a flashlight and examining the inside of Herrod's throat. "There's something here..."

"What is it?" Det. Creed asked.

Mortensen pulled something carefully out of the gash in Thomas's throat and held it up for the others to see. It was a crumpled origami paper crane, once white but now stained red by blood.

"How the hell did you know that would be in his throat?" Det. Creed asked, astounded.

"I know where Draven Crane is," Cosette remarked suddenly.

"Where?" Chief Abberline asked.

"He's my next door neighbor."

"We searched the entire complex and he wasn't there," Creed remarked.

"No one lives on the seventh floor but me. Someone moved in a few weeks ago and I left them a housewarming gift in a tupperware. When they returned the tupperware, it was full of colorful paper cranes just like this one. It has to be him."

"And you didn't think that was important to mention?" Abberline asked.

"As soon as I got it, I found out that Pandora had put my name in the article. It slipped my mind," the girl answered.

"Alright, Det. Creed, Det. Everglow, get a hold of Det. Knox and accompany us to Cosette's apartment. It will just be us, as I don't want to cause a bigger scene in her building. If Crane is there, we'll arrest him as quietly as possible. If he's not, we'll just have to keep searching," the chief said.

"And I can come?" Cosette asked.

"It's your apartment, isn't it?" Creed replied.

When they arrived at Cosette's apartment, Jimmy at the front desk looked rather surprised to see three detectives, the chief, and an FBI agent walk in. Seymour was left to question Jimmy after Agent Abberline got the key to Crane's room from him.

On Abberline's count, Det. Creed, Det. Everglow, and Chief Abberline followed him inside Crane's room. They searched the apartment though they found that it seemed to be completely uninhabited.

"Are you sure someone lives here?" Det. Creed asked.

"Well, I'm pretty sure those paper cranes weren't made by a ghost," Cosette replied.

"That would be crazy," Creed agreed.

"Just like before, he's not here," Chief Abberline said. "Let's go see what Det. Knox found."

Seymour had finished talking with Jimmy when they reached the lobby.

"What did you find, Seymour?" Abberline inquired.

"Well, as it turns out, our alleged 'Draven Crane' *was* here under the name Philip Conners. He rented out the room about two weeks ago."

"About the same time 'Darik Heron' was hired," Det. Everglow recalled.

"Right. Jimmy said that he only ever saw him the day he moved into and out of the apartment and never saw him go in or out any other time," Seymour said.

"He was probably using the fire escape to get in and out," Cosette remarked.

"Did you get a description of this 'Conners?'" the chief asked.

"Yes, and it fits Darik Herron perfectly."

"It must have been pure luck that Crane moved into the same building as Cosette," Agent Abberline said.

"Let's hope so," Cosette muttered.

"Alright, I'm going to have forensics do a sweep on this place, see what they can find because Crane obviously booked it when he figured out we were on his trail," Chief Abberline said.

Cosette spent the rest of that afternoon watching the Mortensens take samples from Crane's apartment and check for blood stains with ultraviolet lights. They actually did find traces of what seemed to be blood in the drains of the sinks and the shower, as well as smudged handprints that could barely be made out on the counter tops and fridge. When they checked inside the fridge they found that it had been left full of food. Some was left over and they had managed to get a couple bite marks and took some samples of the food to see if they couldn't pull DNA from it. They also found several hairs on the cushions of the sofa and bed, but that was all.

Cosette, though, had taken notice of a dripping from the fridge when the freezer had been opened. This reminded her of the freezer at the Hopkins' so she opened it and examined the inside.

"Something's wrong with the freezer," Cosette said, after examining it. "Hey, Creed, help me move this fridge out."

Creed helped her push the refrigerator out into the middle of the floor. Cosette took out her ladybug knife and unscrewed the back of the fridge, pulling the cover off. Stuffed inside the back of the fridge, hidden in the insulation, was a plastic ziplock bag.

"There's something back here," she said, reaching in to pull it out.

She gasped upon seeing the contents.

"What?" the chief asked.

"Det. Everglow," Cosette said. "I believe this is for you."

The detective took the bag from Cosette and gasped in her turn when she saw the contents. Inside was a finger, clearly male, which could only belong to Thomas Herrod. It had turned a sickly greenish purple and looked slimy.

Stuck onto the plastic bag was a gift tag that you would typically find attached to a birthday present. There were even little balloons on it, made demented by the context. On the sticker it read: *To: Det. Eleanor Mary Everglow. From: The Virginia Ripper.*

"Chief, Agent, I think you ought to see this," Everglow said unsteadily.

"Is this Herrod's?" the chief asked upon seeing the finger.

"Yes, it's his missing finger," Cosette said grimly. "It's also a threat. He is letting us know that he means to kill Det. Everglow."

"So the fish bit the lure, huh?" Det. Creed said.

"Clearly," Cosette said.

"Alright, then let's catch this bastard before anything else can happen," the head-detective growled.

Chapter Twenty-Three:

Agent Abberline had decided that it would be unwise for Cosette to remain in her apartment seeing as how Crane knew where she lived. Cosette didn't seem opposed to leaving her apartment while they searched for Crane, so he took that chance to contact Dr. Vale.

"I have a favor to ask of you," Abberline remarked when Vale answered the phone.

"Alright, shoot," she replied.

"The Crane knows where Cosette lives. As it turns out, he was living across from her this whole time. It's too dangerous for her to be in her apartment anymore. Do you think she could stay with you for a while?"

Dr. Vale sighed.

"If I couldn't take her as a patient, what makes you think I could board her?"

"All she's doing is staying in your house where Crane won't be able to find her. It's just until we can find her somewhere more suitable."

"And there isn't anyone else who could take her?"

"I'm not certain she would be comfortable with anyone else, and I can't have her running away. You've known her the longest, and surely she trusts you the most."

"Alright, as long as you think she would be safe with me," Vale agreed at last.

"Thank you. I'll bring her over in just a bit."

Cosette seemed to have it in her head that she was to stay in a hotel until the Crane had been apprehended, and though she was annoyed with the idea of having to share a space with someone, she releuctantly packed her bags, put Magnolia in her crate, and went with Abberline to Dr. Vale's house, which was not too far from the university.

"Hello, Arnold, Cosette. I'm glad you're alright. Come in. Can I get you anything to drink?" Dr. Vale asked when they arrived.

When both of them declined, Vale said to Cosette, "Well, let me show you to the guest room so you can put your things away. They look heavy."

She led Cosette up stairs to a cozy bedroom with floral purple wallpaper. Cosette set her bag at the foot of the bed and let Magnolia, who was meowing angrily, out of her crate.

When Cosette had settled and seemed comfortable, Dr. Vale asked the director, "Would you like to stay for supper? It's nearly ready."

"Oh, no, I'm quite alright. Carol will be furious if I miss her three cheese shrimp parm surprise."

"Oh, she'll have to give me the recipe," Dr. Vale said.

"She's never given it to anyone," Abberline laughed. "Only she and her mother ever knew what was in it."

"And you're sure Cosette will be alright here?" Vale asked suddenly, looking back to the living room where Cosette, holding the cat, was inspecting the bookshelves.

"She should be fine. If either of you need anything at all, just call," Abberline answered.

He left after saying goodbye to Cosette. Dr. Vale busied herself with finishing supper. Cosette entered and stood on the other side of the marble counter, watching her uncertainly.

"Who is this?" Dr. Vale asked, nodding to the cat.

"Magnolia. I got her from a pound near where I used to sleep. No one wanted her, so they were going to murder her," Cosette replied.

"What do you mean where you used to sleep?" Dr. Vale asked.

"Well, I was homeless for a while, obviously. I couldn't just go to a shelter; they would have put me in a program or something."

"Oh dear, I'm so sorry that happened to you."

Cosette shrugged.

"It builds character. And *characters* at that. Makes my stories more interesting. You don't mind having cats around, of course?"

"Oh, no, in fact, I have a tabby cat, Fydor. He should be around here somewhere."

"What are you making?" Cosette asked, watching as the woman stirred a pot on the stove.

"Cheesy chicken pasta—my mom's comfort recipe, some roast garlic soup, bread, and white chocolate and macadamia nut cookies. Apart from teaching psychology, I do consider myself a bit of a master chef," Dr. Vale remarked with a smile.

Cosette was sitting on the doctor's couch watching the television while working on the latest chapter in which she met with Herrod, when there came a knock on her door. She sat up, alert. Dr. Vale had gone to her classes at the university early that morning leaving Cosette alone and was not due back until late. She hadn't said anyone was meant to come that afternoon.

She got up and walked to the door, peering through the spy hole in the door to see Dr. Carnifex on the other side, and opened the door.

"Hello, Doctor. I didn't forget a session, did I?" Cosette asked.

"Not at all. I heard about what happened with the Crane

and I wanted to make sure you were alright. Arnold said you were staying with Dr. Vale, so I brought you supper," Dr. Carnifex said, holding up a tin pan covered in aluminum.

"Thank you. Would you like to come in—or something?" the girl asked.

She let the doctor in and he set the pan on the counter. He was met with Magnolia, who jumped up on the counter and insisted on prying at the aluminum covering.

"Hello, Magnolia," the doctor said, picking the cat up and setting her down on the floor. "She is quite an interesting cat."

Thank you," Cosette replied. "By the way, can I get you anything to eat or drink?"

"No thank you, I'm quite alright," the doctor answered. "But how about you?"

"Me? I suppose I'm a little thirsty," the girl replied.

"I mean are you alright?" the doctor clarified. "Mentally."

"Oh, yeah, I'm fine," Cosette answered.

"Are you certain? You've seemed troubled lately."

"I'm assisting in solving a murder; of course I seem troubled," the girl responded.

"Does this case bother you? Is that why you've been having these nightmares?"

"I always have nightmares, Doctor."

"Do you feel safe living alone, Cosette?"

"I'm really fine."

"I wonder if you really know the meaning of that word."

"This isn't another session, Doctor," Costte remarked sternly.

"You shouldn't bury your feelings."

"I don't like to talk about my ridiculous feelings," Cosette remarked.

"It is not a weakness to show vulnerability, you know," the doctor returned.

Cosette frowned.

What was strangest to her was that this was not an argument. It was not an altercation. It was simply the doctor expressing his concern for her. It was quite unlike anything she had experienced with her aunt and uncle.

"There is one thing I'm concerned about," Cosette admitted. "During Herrod's autopsy, they found a paper crane in his throat."

"The Crane making his presence known, perhaps?"

Cosette left him and went up to her bedroom. She retrieved the box of paper cranes, which she had kept, and sat it in front of him, handing him the note that had been included.

"I received these after I gifted the neighbor, who was allegedly Draven Crane, a housewarming gift."

"The same cranes," the doctor inspected.

"And the worst part is that I never told him my name."

"This must be very frightening for you."

"No. I'm not frightened. I'm expectant," the girl replied.

"Of what?"

"I'm not sure if you're aware of this, Doctor, but, despite my lacking beauty, I have resemblance to the women he killed. I fit the profile as well."

"You think the Crane will come after you?" Dr. Carnifex asked.

"If he doesn't go after Det. Everglow."

"But he doesn't know where you are."

"Just because I'm residing with Dr. Vale doesn't mean that I'm invincible," Cosette said. "He could find me if he wanted."

"Have you discussed this with Arnold?"

"He knows of the paper cranes, but not of my concerns. It would be arrogant of me to assume that I have a serial killer after me. Besides, he would say that they already set it up so that Crane would come after Everglow."

"What is the difference between Crane's feelings towards you and those towards Det. Everglow?"

"He feels something close to friendliness towards me, though he dislikes Det. Everglow, yet he still finds interest in her."

"And those feelings could potentially be dangerous?" the

doctor asked.

"Yes. I think it could be."

When Dr. Carnifex had gone, Cosette peeked under the aluminum foil to see what was inside the pan. It was homemade lasagna. Deciding that she was hungry, she went to get a plate down. She set it down on the counter and turned to grab a knife to cut a slice when she heard a scratching coming from upstairs, specifically the guest bedroom, like the window was being opened.

Someone was coming into Dr. Vale's house uninvited.

Wielding the knife she had meant to cut the lasagna with, she tiptoed to the bedroom. The door was only open a crack but she could still see inside.

The window was wide open, but she couldn't see if anyone was inside the room or not. She decided that she was going to have to bust in on the count of three and stab whatever came at her.

One...

Two...

Three!

She burst in and was immediately grabbed and thrown across the room by an unseen attacker, losing the knife in the process. She regained herself only enough to recognize her attacker as Draven Crane before he grabbed her and pressed a wet handkerchief over her nose.

She knew it was drenched in chloroform, she was a writer for God's sake. But she was still human, and if she didn't breathe, she would pass out from suffocation.

At last, despite her struggling, the chloroform set in, and darkness overtook her.

❀❀❀

When Dr. Vale returned home, she called for Cosette, although she received no answer. Of course, Cosette didn't usually answer her unless she felt like it. There was an aluminum pan of food on the counter, though she wondered why Cosette hadn't put it in the fridge. Entering the living room she found that

Cosette was not there, nor was she in the dining room. She usually ate in the guest bedroom if she ate anyway, so she wasn't too concerned. But when she went upstairs she saw the guest bedroom door was wide open. The girl was not inside, though the window was open, and Magnolia stood meowing sadly at it. A kitchen knife lay in the corner of the room and there were signs of a struggle.

Panicked, Dr. Vale rushed around her house, searching and calling out for Cosette, though she only found Magnolia under the sofa. She dug her phone out of her purse and wasted no time in calling Agent Abberline.

"She's *gone*?" Abberline exclaimed. "Gone *where*?"

"I don't know. I just got back from my last session and she isn't here. There are signs of struggling in her room. You don't think the Crane found her?"

"Shit," the director groaned.

"What?" came the chief's voice in the background.

"Cosette disappeared from Vale's house. She thinks Crane got her."

"You said he wouldn't find her here!" Vale exclaimed.

"It's going to be fine. Carol's sending squad cars out now, and I'm going to see if I can't reach her somehow."

"I'm coming down to the station right now," Dr. Vale said.

"No, I'll come to you. I should have the room inspected anyway."

"I've tried calling her *ten times*!" Vale remarked when the director arrived.

"Let's see her room," Abberline said.

Vale took him upstairs and he saw the room in its disarray.

"She definitely put up a fight," he said.

He went to look out the open window where the sorry cat still sat and saw that Crane must have climbed up the storm drain to reach the window and likely escaped the same way. As he looked around the room he noticed to his dismay a baby blue paper crane sitting on the bookshelf.

"No," Abberline whispered in dismay.

❀❀❀

Chief Abberline directed officers to different parts of the town to search for Cosette beginning from the outskirts in and blocking to roads in hopes of rescuing her before it was too late.

"Chief, what's going on?" Det. Creed asked, entering her office.

"Cosette was taken by the Crane," the chief replied.

"What?" came Det. Everglow, who had followed him.

"The Crane's kidnapped Cosette," Creed responded.

"What!" Everglow exclaimed. "But why would he go after Cosette? *I* was the one who was used as bait."

"Apparently she was unknowingly nice to him," the chief remarked. "And Pandora put her name in the article. Crane must have read it before she could revise it."

"Well, we haven't any time to waste," Everglow remarked. "We have to find Cosette before it's too late!"

"I have officers out looking now," the chief said.

"Well, I intend to help. She got kidnapped in my place. That's my fault. I mean to find her."

Chapter Twenty-Four:

Cosette woke slowly. Her vision was blurred, and she felt rather dizzy and disoriented. She blinked her eyes until she could see clearly again and looked around herself to figure out her surroundings.

When everything had settled itself, she found that she was lying on a bed in an unfamiliar room. She sat up, her head swimming, and tried to stand but found that her wrist was handcuffed to the headboard. She pulled at it groggily, but it really didn't do much except jingle.

"Ah, there you are," said an unfamiliar voice.

Cosette spun around to look around at the unknown speaker. There, bending down at the bedside, was Draven Crane.

"Crane!" Cosette gasped.

She had the idea to leap from the bed but recalled that her wrist was still locked to the bed.

"Oh, no, you won't be going anywhere, my dear Cosette," Crane said.

He then drew very close to her, examining her face, before he tucked some of her loose hair back into place. Cosette flinched back and slapped his hand away.

"Don't touch me!" the girl exclaimed.

His demeanor fell.

"Of course, I suppose it wouldn't be the first hurtful thing you've said about me."

"What are you talking about?" Cosette asked in confusion, her head still hurting from the chloroform.

"Oh, you know. All those things you put in that shoddy tabloid newspaper. You think I'm a pervert? You think I hurt my victims?"

"No, you just kill them," Cosette replied sardonically.

"Tell me, Cosette, why would you say all that about me after being so kind to me?" Crane asked imploringly.

"Well, first of all, I didn't say *all that* about you. I simply said that you were sexually attracted to the particular women you kill—mostly to save your dignity—that you were a heartless monster and a sexual deviant, as well as being completely unoriginal, having stolen your murder tactics off Mr. Herrod, and that you had probably killed your wife because you cheated on her," Cosette elucidated.

"But that makes no *sense*! You *know* none of that's true! I know you know!" Crane pressed.

"Of course none of it's true," Cosette agreed.

"So you don't believe all that nonsense?"

"Not at all. We only said all of that to try and bait you; to lure you out. We purposely said things that would infuriate you so you might slip up and reveal yourself."

"That was really rather clever," Crane admitted.

"Of course, you already revealed yourself, didn't you?" Cosette said. "When you killed Mr. Herrod and stuffed that paper crane down his throat."

"Yes, that's right. I wanted you to see me. I—I wanted them all to see me," Crane said, drawing a chair from the corner of the room and sitting down beside the bed. "I wanted them to know that I am not a Copycat."

"Who are you then?" Cosette asked.

"I am Draven Crane," Crane replied. "I am *The* Crane!"

"Why did you kill your wife, Mr. Crane? Why did you kill those women?"

Crane stopped and looked at Cosette with wide eyes, as if she had slapped him.

"I had to," Crane said finally, twisting his fingers together.

"Why?" the girl asked.

"Because *he* was going to kill her!"

"Who was?" Cosette asked interestedly.

"My father."

"But you're father's dead," Cosette remarked.

"No, he isn't. I can hear him. Every night. He shouts, and stomps around the house, and bangs on the door. He haunts my dreams and my reality, and I never can tell the difference anymore. Sometimes I don't sleep for entire nights. But he's there... he's there...I can hear his drunken voice calling out to me at night.

"He says he'll kill Nora. He says he'll kill me. I'll see women who look like Nora. Father...he is so determined to ruin my life, to finish what he said he would do...he forgets that Nora's dead. He forgets what he made me do, so he says he's going to kill them. He'll shout and he'll shout, and he'll shout, and he'll shout...And I just know I have to protect them. I've got to protect them from him the way nobody ever protected *me* from that crazy bastard."

"By killing them?" Cosette asked. "Do you know how backwards that is?"

"What do you mean?" Crane asked harshly.

"It's insane, that's what I mean," Cosette said.

"Insane?" Crane exclaimed, his voice rising. "Do you even know what insane *is*? *Insane* is the time my father tried to suffocate me when he was drunk. *Insane* is the time my father nearly choked me to death. *Insane* is my father promising to kill my wife. And my mother, the only person I ever had to look to for protection, stepped back. She stepped aside. She never stopped him!

"So when he promised that he would get me someday—that he would kill me—I knew he meant it, in life or in death, I knew he meant it. And I don't care; he can try and kill me if he wants, and he may very well. But I won't let him have Nora, and I won't let him have those poor women who didn't do anything wrong."

Cosette realized that she was being rude and that being rude wouldn't get her anywhere but dead. This man clearly thought his wicked deeds were "noble". He thought he was rescuing those women by killing them. Rescuing them from his own suffering. She was going to have to let her empathy get the better of her this time around, even if the man *was* a serial killer.

"That must have been terrible for you," Cosette remarked sympathetically.

"You have no idea," Crane said quietly, shaking his head.

"Well, I know that I'll only ever be able to imagine your pain. But then again, you'll only ever be able to imagine mine," Cosette said.

"What do you mean?"

"You know, this isn't the first time someone has tried to kill me before."

"I'm not going to kill you, Cosette," Crane assured her. "I'm going to protect you."

"Ah, right," Cosette nodded, wondering if those two words meant the same thing to him.

"Who tried to kill you?" Crane asked.

"Antony Sanguini, a serial killer also known as the Northeast Nightmare," Cosette answered.

Crane looked very startled and muttered, "I ought to kill him."

"You needn't."

"Why? Don't tell me you 'forgave' him and all that nonsense."

"No," the girl replied, shaking her head. "I killed him myself."

Crane went quiet and simply examined the girl. Cosette

was terribly uncomfortable in her turn, as she hated being stared at.

"You know, Nora and I tried for a child. If Nora and I had had a child, she would've been about your age. I bet she would've been just like you," Crane remarked, cocking his head to the side.

"Oh, I hope not," Cosette replied.

"What do you mean?" Cosette asked.

"Let's just say I'm not a model daughter."

"There's no such thing as a model daughter. Or frankly a model son. I think we'll all disappoint ourselves until we realize that we can never be perfect for other people."

"Do you know that you can't please your father?"

"I don't want to please him," Crane remarked. "I want to protect everyone from him."

"You won't hurt anyone from the article will you? Now that you know it was all just a ploy?" Cosette asked.

Crane didn't answer but sat there in silence for a while before he stood and moved the chair back against the wall beside the nightstand.

"I've got to go. If you'll excuse me," Crane said at last.

Crane left the room and Cosette heard his footsteps disappear down the stairs. As soon as he was gone, she took her decorative butterfly bobby pin out of her hair with her free hand and went about trying to pick the lock on the cuff.

"Shame," Cosette muttered, as she bent the pin into shape. "I liked this one."

Downstairs, Crane went into the kitchen and dialed a number into his phone. It ran for a while before the other end picked up.

"Hello?" Det. Everglow answered. "Hello?"

Crane didn't answer for a moment.

"You seem to have lost something," Crane said.

"Who is this?" Det. Everglow asked sharply.

"Oh, surely you're clever enough to have figured that out by now," Crane answered.

"Crane," Everglow breathed. "Where is Cosette?"

"Oh, surely you can figure that out as well. And when you do, come alone. For Cosette's sake," Crane added.

"Don't you do anything to her, do you hear me?" Det. Everglow exclaimed.

"That completely depends on you," Crane returned.

Then he hung up. When he went back upstairs, he found that Cosette had just unlocked the cuff and managed to get free. She looked surprised seeing as how she had expected him to take longer.

"Um...it was too tight," she excused.

"That's fine. I was just about to let you out," Crane replied.

"Really?"

"Of course. I don't want you to be uncomfortable. Besides, you wouldn't find your way out anyhow; we're in the middle of nowhere. It's nothing but miles of trees and roads. You wouldn't get far in the dark."

"Who did you call?"

Crane didn't reply.

Chapter Twenty-Five:

Det. Everglow tried to dial the number again but the man wouldn't pick up again. Her first instinct was to get a hold of Det. Creed and the Abberlines and tell them this new information, but then she realized that she would ultimately be putting Cosette's life in even more danger than it was already in. So instead, she hurried over to her computer and hurriedly traced the call. She thought she might not be able to track it seeing as how the call had already ended, but she found that Crane had his GPS on.

She pinpointed the location of the call, which was apparently from out in the middle of nowhere.

She knew that she shouldn't go alone. Crane wanted her to come, he was expecting her. He probably meant to kill her. Of course, she was a brilliant shot, but Crane might be as well, and for all she knew, he was the type of serial killer who wasn't all that interested in toying with his victims first.

She picked up her gun, which hung on her belt on the back of the chair and checked it to make sure it had bullets in it.

"Det. Everglow?"

Everglow jumped and spun around to face Seymour Knox.

"Oh, Seymour, what are you still doing here? I thought everyone went home?"

"You aren't going to go alone, are you?"

"Of course I'm going home alone, Seymour," Det. Everglow lied.

"I was standing at the fax room door when Crane called. I heard everything," Det. Knox answered.

"You can't tell anyone about this," Det. Everglow ordered sharply.

"You aren't really just going to go busting into a serial killer's house without backup?"

"I can handle myself. Thank you for your concern."

"He wants to kill you."

"He wants to kill Cosette, too."

"That's exactly why you shouldn't go alone."

"This may be the only chance we get to save Cosette and stop the Crane; I'm not passing that up," Det. Everglow said determinedly. "And if you try to stop me or tell anyone about this, woe be unto you."

Seymour realized he couldn't stop Everglow from doing exactly what she had set her mind to, so he watched as she left the station and went out to her car. When he had seen her drive away he sighed and dialed Det. Creed on his phone.

❀❀❀

"She's *what*?" Creed shouted when Seymour told him all that had happened. "Why didn't you stop her?"

"I tried, but she wouldn't listen so I thought you could try and talk some sense into her."

"I'm calling Abberline, and I'm coming to the station immediately," Creed remarked before hanging up.

Everglow was already a good way into the country when her phone began to ring. She saw it was Creed and ignored it, but after seven more times of him ringing, she picked it up.

"Now, you listen here, Eleanor, you turn around right now, and come back to the station before you get yourself killed," Creed barked.

"Crane has Cosette. If I don't go, he might *kill* her before we can get to her," Everglow replied.

"And if you go alone, he'll kill both of you," Creed said.

"You should come back, and we can plan this out strategically."

"I'm already almost there. I'm not turning back now," Det. Everglow remarked.

And with that she hung up. Det. Creed tried to call her again, but she wouldn't answer, so he slammed his phone down on the desk before picking it up and dialing Agent Abberline.

"Crane got in contact with Eleanor and told her to meet him," Creed said.

"She didn't go, did she?"

"Apparently she's 'already almost there and she's not turning back now.'"

"Damn it. I thought she would be the sensible partner."

"What's that supposed to mean?"

"I'll call S.W.A.T on the way over to the station. And Dr. Vale as well. She might be able to help us with Crane. Try and find out where she's headed."

"Already did," Seymour said. "She tracked the call and left it up on her computer; all I had to do was hack the computer's password to access it all."

"Wow, and here I was thinking you were an idiot," Det. Creed remarked, though Seymour glared at him in offense.

When Det. Everglow reached the forest, there was no sign of anyone else there. Of course, Crane wouldn't make things *that* easy. Taking out her gun, she cocked it, ready to fire at anything that attacked.

She entered into the forest with the utmost caution. Everything was silent and she began to wonder if Crane was even waiting for her or if he was just trying to rile the police.

She had made her way deep into the forest when she felt a sudden chill on the back of her neck as though someone was watching her. She looked around, though she didn't see anything. She was just walking on again when she heard a rustling behind her. She didn't show any sign that she knew she was being pursued in an attempt to lure him out.

Again she heard the rustling at her side now, though

again, no one was there.

"I know you're there! Go ahead and come out!" Det. Everglow called into the darkness.

There was the sound of someone running through the trees and without any hesitation, Everglow took off after him.

Once or twice the figure of a man, though she couldn't quite make him out in the darkness. Finally all was silent in the depths of the woods. She looked around again and took notice of something lying at the base of a nearby tree. She went over to it and saw that it was a blue sweater.

She picked it up and examined it, wide-eyed in concern. It looked like Cosette's. She hurriedly tucked it into her purse, growing ever more worried about the missing girl's safety. It was then that she realized that she didn't quite know where she was.

She decided to go back a ways and try to find her way back through the dense trees back to the main road. After a while of walking without any luck, she heard a sudden shout.

"Eleanor!"

Det. Everglow spun around to see Det. Creed running towards her, Det. Knox, the Abberlines and the S.W.A.T team following close behind.

"Eleanor, what the hell are you thinking?" Det. Creed barked angrily.

"Haven't I told you enough? He said that he would harm Cosette if I didn't show up," Det. Everglow returned.

"But you didn't even consult me first!"

"I don't need your permission to save a life."

"Of course you don't, but you shouldn't chase killers alone!"

"Why, because I'm a woman and need a 'big, strong man' to protect me?" Everglow shouted.

"No, because I don't want to lose you like I lost Angelo!" Creed shouted in return, grabbing her by the shoulders and shaking her.

Det. Everglow stared at him, taken aback. The head-detective sighed and rubbed a hand over his eyes.

"I just don't want to fail anyone else," he remarked.

"You didn't fail anyone, Alastor—"

"No, I did. But I won't fail you too. We're partners, after all. That means we do this together. You're not dying without me, got it?"

"Okay, okay, you're right," Det. Everglow agreed, smiling softly. "We should find the Crane together; as partners."

Det. Creed smiled in his turn and rubbed the back of his neck.

"Alright. Enough of this chick-flick sap. Did you find any clues that could point to Crane?"

"Um, yes, actually. I think this is Cosette's sweater," Det. Everglow said, taking it out of her bag and holding it up for him to see.

"That would mean he definitely has her then," Creed said, furrowing his brow.

"If anything happens to her because of me—"

"Nothing's going to happen to her. She's a smart kid; she'll be alright," Det. Creed assured her, though he wasn't convinced himself.

❀❀❀

They searched the forest up and down and wherever Det. Everglow remarked that she thought to have seen the figure who was allegedly the Crane. They looked all night, but they found no sign of a house let alone people. They supposed that Crane had made a run for it after realizing that the FBI had actually picked up his trail, or else he had intended for them to find nothing but the sweater.

When the sun had begun to rise over the horizon, they had decided to call the search off and returned to the station, weary and with shadows darkening under their eyes.

They took the sweater to the Mortensens for inspection as soon as they had come in. The Mortensens got to work on the evidence right away and had gotten the results ready by lunch time, though it was exactly what the two detectives had been both dreading and expecting.

"So, I was able to match the DNA—obviously it's hardly complicated to extract and match DNA if you know how to do it. It's simple really—"

"Mortensen," Creed interrupted shortly. "Whose DNA is it?"

"Believe it or not it is someone we know—"

"Mortensen, just spit it out!" Creed exclaimed exasperatedly.

"Oh, yes, yes, my apologies. It's Cosette's DNA," Mortensen replied.

"I knew it. Crane really does have her," Det. Everglow said. "You don't think he harmed Cosette, do you? Is that what this sweater is supposed to mean?"

"He's warning us to keep ourselves at bay," Det. Creed remarked.

"Ugh, I never would have done that article if I had known Cosette would get even more mixed up in all this."

"It's my fault for not doing an extra check on what Pandora had written and Pandora's fault for writing it," Agent Abberline said.

"Oh, don't worry. She'll get what's coming to her," Everglow assured him.

"So, how are we supposed to find Cosette?" Chief Abberline asked.

"I'm sending people to search that entire forest all over again," Abberline said. "But other than that, we just have to wait until we can get more leads."

Chapter Twenty-Six:

Cosette had woken late that morning and felt her heart drop when she realized that none of what had occurred had been just another bad dream.

She found that the bathroom connected to the bedroom was supplied with feminine bath products, some half used, towels, and a hair dryer, straightener and curling iron. She also found clothing in the closet that was similar to her own size, so she put them on, seeing as how her clothes had become rather dirty.

She wondered if the bath supplies and clothes had been put there by Crane specifically for her, and if so, how long he had been stalking her, or if they had been there before her, and if they had, who they had belonged to. She hoped the clothes hadn't belonged to one of his victims.

She could almost laugh to herself thinking of how crazy it was that she had gotten kidnapped because of baked goods and a newspaper article. It was definitely the last time she ever left a gift basket for anyone. In fact, she was about ready to start looking for a new apartment.

She knew that she wouldn't be able to hide in the bedroom forever, especially if she intended to ever escape from Crane. At last, Crane came up and knocked on the door. Cosette was hesitant to answer the door, but at last Crane simply walked in.

"Cosette, are you in here?" he asked.

"Oh, yes—yes, I was just dressing, I didn't hear you," the girl lied. "Did you need something?"

"I just wanted to tell you that breakfast is nearly ready."

"Oh, thank you. I'll be down in just a minute."

Crane returned to the kitchen, and Cosette composed herself a little more, preparing herself to pacify the killer until she could find an escape, before following him.

She stood hesitantly in the kitchen doorway until Crane said, "Come sit down, Cosette."

She took a seat at one of the stools at the marble island and watched as Crane flipped pancakes and bacon in the pan. Finally he put the bacon, eggs, sausage, and a pancake doused in syrup on a plate and set it in front of her, seating himself across from her. Cosette didn't even pick up her fork.

"Are you not hungry?" Crane asked.

Cosette shook her head.

"Ah, I see. It's alright. I know this sort of thing can be rather overwhelming," Crane said.

There was a moment of silence, which was only broken by the clinking of the man's knife and fork.

"Could I ask who lived here before me?" Cosette asked.

"Who says anyone lived here before you?"

"The upstairs bathroom and wardrobe are supplied. Of course, that could be for me, but why would some of the soap bottles be half empty then? So someone must have been here before me."

Crane tapped the side of his plate with his fork.

"This was Nora and my house after we first got married," he remarked. "I wanted to live in the middle of nowhere, so people couldn't find us. She wanted to move into the city, though, so of course I did for her. When it was put on the market by my mother, I rebought it under an alias."

"I see. And I suppose that no one is looking for me?"

"Of course there are people looking for you, Cosette. I have the whole Bureau in a frenzy searching for you," Crane answered.

"Will they find me?"

"I don't think so."

"You know you can't keep me a prisoner forever."

"You're not a prisoner," Crane remarked.

"Then what am I?"

"This is your new home, Cosette."

"What are you talking about?"

"You have no place. Like me. You can stay here. You finally have a home."

"You're a wanted killer," Cosette remarked. "And dead to boat."

"That means little to people like us."

"Have you ever thought about seeing a psychologist?" the girl asked, the smallest idea forming in the back of her mind.

"I don't go to them anymore after I moved out of my mother's house," Crane replied.

"I stopped seeing them too after I moved out of my aunt and uncle's house. But Abberline–the agent, not the chief of police—set me up with one—Dr. Carnifex, and he's wonderful. I've felt so much better since I've started going. I'm actually supposed to have an appointment in two days," Cosette remarked.

"You aren't really *wanting* to go to that appointment, are you?" the man asked.

"I think I ought to. I'd hate to ruin my progress. And it isn't like I'll run away. Don't you trust me?" she asked innocently.

"No," Crane answered flatly.

❀❀❀

Crane had taken up a job as a mechanic after killing his last victim. Before that, he had worked at a bar. To go to his job, he had to leave Cosette alone.

Cosette had been sitting in an armchair, examining one of the books off one of Crane's bookshelves when he approached her.

"I'm going to lock you in your room," he remarked.

"What? Why?" Cosette asked in confusion.

"I have to go to work, and I don't want you trying anything," Crane answered.

"Where do you work?" the girl asked.

"A mechanic shop in town."

"How long does it take you to get there?"

"A good while by car, and much longer by foot," the man replied, pulling on his jacket.

He then pulled Cosette upstairs to her bedroom and shut and locked her inside. Cosette didn't put up a fight. She just needed him to leave.

He had gone away soon enough. Cosette waited until he had been gone about thirty minutes before she took her bobby pin out from where she had hidden it under the mattress and picked the lock on the door. It took her a while to get it open, but eventually she did and made her way downstairs.

She looked around the house for anything to defend herself with in case she ran into the Crane again. When she got to the front door, she found that all she had to do to get out was unlock the door.

She went to turn the lock, but as soon as she touched the handle, she felt a shock travel through her body and the next thing she knew, she hit the floor.

❀❀❀

When Cosette woke, she was lying on the couch in the living room with a pillow under her head and a blanket over her shoulders. She heard the television going and slowly opened her eyes, feeling a strange prickling in her limbs, and saw that some cop show was playing. After a minute she pushed herself into a sitting position and looked around.

She saw Crane sitting in the armchair in front of the television, a beer and the remote in hand. She watched him cautiously, wondering what she should do. That was when he spoke.

"You got out."

"What?" Cosette asked groggily, rubbing her aching temples.

"You tried to *escape*," Crane growled.

"Yeah, well, you kidnapped me. What did you expect me to do?" the girl returned.

Crane slammed his beer down on the table, causing Cosette to flinch.

"When I locked you in that room and told you to stay there, you were meant to do as I told you!"

"I can't help that I want to go home—"

Crane struck Cosette across the face so hard that her head snapped to the side, and blood trickled down her cheek. She looked up at the killer, rather shocked.

"I won't punish you this time, but take this as a fair warning. If you ever try to escape again, I will make certain that you regret it," Crane hissed. "Go to your room."

Cosette was more than glad to put distance between herself and the killer. She quietly shut the door behind her and sunk onto the bed, pulling her legs close to her chest. What if no one ever found her? Crane was insane, and she knew that, sooner or later, he would get it in his head to kill her.

He had said he had the whole FBI out looking for her. Surely they were looking for her even now if that was so. If she couldn't find a way to escape, and if the FBI couldn't find her, maybe she could convince Crane to go to Dr. Carnifex for a counseling session, and maybe he would even bring her along, and the doctor could go to Abberline. But he had been very against that idea when she had suggested it.

Crane called Cosette down for supper, and she hesitantly came down. Crane was just taking the pork out of the oven. He looked up as she entered.

"Ah, there you are, Cosette. Mind putting together the salad while I finish the roast? The vegetables are washed in the sink."

Cosette didn't have a choice in the matter, she knew, so she went over and took the bowl of vegetables out of the sink.

"Here," Crane said.

He reached over and took a knife from the block on the other side of the girl. She flinched when he did so. This did not get past Crane and he frowned, examining the girl's face.

"You're bleeding," he remarked, brushing the cut he himself had given her.

"It's fine," Cosette muttered, pulling away.

"Let me mend it for you."

Crane went to one of the cupboards and took out a medical kit. He got out alcohol and bandages, cleaning the cuts and the burns on her hands from the electrified door knob. The cleaning alcohol was cold and it stung, but the aloe he put on her hands for the electrical burns was soothing. She wanted to draw away from the man who was too close but restrained herself until he had finished applying the bandage on the cuts.

Cosette found it strange how Crane could switch from furious and violent, to amiable and kind in just a few hours. Of course, she knew this was due to his mental instability which led to his violent outbursts. She knew this thing wasn't unusual in psychotic killers; it was just more frightening when it was your life hanging on the line.

"You know I only hurt you because I had to, right?" Crane asked, patting the bandage on her cheek. "I just want you to be safe, and it isn't safe to leave right now. At least not yet."

"That's alright," Cosette said quietly, hoping to appease him with what he wanted to hear.

Supper was very quiet, and Cosette couldn't bring herself to eat, but picked at her food, occasionally nibbling on a bit of something.

"You ought to eat, you know. It's been almost two days since you've eaten something."

"I don't feel too well," she admitted.

"Oh, well, don't make yourself eat anything then."

Crane finished his meal soon enough and had Cosette join him in front of the television where he proceeded to fall asleep. Cosette knew it was far too risky to try to escape, especially with the killer in the same room.

There were two line phones in the house though. One was on the kitchen wall and the other was in Crane's bedroom. She tiptoed upstairs after she was certain the man was asleep, and hurriedly dialed Agent Abberline's phone. It rang momentarily, then the director answered.

"Hello? Who is it?"

"Abberline, it's me," she whispered.

"Cosette? Are you alright? Where are you?"

"I'm fine for now, but I haven't the slightest idea where I am. Crane jumped me in my apartment and took me to the house he used to live in with his wife. All I know is that there's a forest surrounding the place and apparently it's in the middle of nowhere. I tried to get out, but he electrocuted the doors and I got caught. He's sleeping now, but I don't have much time. You have to trace this call and find me."

"I'm at home right now. Try and stay on long enough for me to get to the office and track you," Abberline said, pulling on his pants. "Crane hasn't hurt you has he?"

"No," Cosette replied. "I'm alright."

"Okay, that's good. I'm getting in my car right now," the director remarked.

"Oh, and another thing that might be helpful is that he said he works at a mechanic shop in town," Cosette asked. "Just in case you can't track me here."

"Don't be ridiculous. We'll find you, no doubt."

Abberline told Cosette to stay on the line until he could get to his computer. She listened to the purr of his car through the phone. He announced when he arrived at the station and she had just heard the door clang shut when there was a scream from downstairs. Cosette flinched.

"I have to go," she told Abberline urgently.

"Cosette, wait—"

Cosette slipped the phone back down into its holder and hurried to her bedroom, slipping under the sheets. She pretended to be asleep just as she heard Crane's footsteps on the stairs.

Chapter Twenty-Seven:

Crane had been sleeping peacefully in his chair, completely unaware of Cosette's phone call upstairs. That was, until he heard tapping. It was a soft, rhythmic tapping at first, then it grew faster and louder until it was akin to the drumming of Crane heart in his ears. He trembled at the sound as beads of perspiration began to form on his forehead and trickled down his temples.

He knew what this meant. He tried to move, but his muscles were limp. He couldn't call out to anyone. Not his mother, not Nora—Nora. Nora was dead. Nora was lying, bleeding on the floor. Her wide open eyes staring up at him.

Up at him?

He was standing now, in the kitchen. The room swayed. Nora was dead. Who would do such a terrible thing as to kill his Nora?

"You stupid son of a bitch!"

Crane spun around to meet his father, glowering at him, a bottle in hand.

"Look what you've done! The mess you've made!"

Crane looked around himself and saw that the kitchen was covered in blood.

"No, I—I didn't!" Crane stammered, stepping back.

"God, I told you I'd kill her...Didn't know you would do it for me," his father growled, chuckling and drinking from his liquor bottle.

"I said I didn't!" Crane exclaimed.

"So who was it then?"

"Y—you...it was you!"

"You're such a coward that you can't even admit that you killed that whore," Mr. Crane grumbled, wiping his mouth with the back of his hand.

"Don't talk about Nora like that!" Crane cried.

"What are you gonna do, boy?" his father scoffed.

Crane felt his shoulders slump.

"That's what I thought," his father nodded, taking another swig. "You're not a real man. Can't stand up to me. You know what I'm gonna do? I'm gonna take everything from you."

"You already killed Nora," Crane remarked.

"Not *Nora*...No, not *Nora*," Mr. Crane shook his head. "You know what I'll do? I'll kill dear *Cosette*."

"No, you can't!"

"What are you gonna do to stop me?" his father sneered. "Just like you stopped me from killing all those other broads? Did a real good job putting 'em in the ground for me."

"She could've been mine and Nora's. She could've been ours if you hadn't killed Nora!"

"You killed Nora."

"You made me kill her!"

"You did it all on your own; just like you killed all those other girls."

"I didn't, I didn't, I *didn't*!" Crane shouted, shaking his head vigorously.

"I'll kill Cosette."

"No..."

Then Crane felt blow after blow striking his skin. His

father hit him over and over. Finally, it stopped and Crane found himself on the floor, looking up at his father's great, beet-colored face.

"I'll kill her!"

"No."

"I'll kill her!" his father said, drawing a knife from the block on the counter.

"No!" Crane screamed.

❀❀❀

He woke with a jolt and a shout. Without another thought, he ran up the stairs into the bedroom in which Cosette resided and hurriedly shook her awake.

"Cosette, we have to go," he urged.

"Go? Where?" Cosette asked uncertainly, looking up at Crane.

His face was bruised and bloody and he looked terrified.

"Carnifex—where does he live?"

"I don't know where he lives; I only know where he works," Cosette answered.

"Alright, that's perfect, let's go. We've got to go."

Crane dragged her out of bed and down the stairs out to the car. They drove down the long dirt path that led to the road, and Cosette noticed that there was a mailbox, the reflective numbers on it shimmering in the moonlight.

They drove in silence together in the darkness along the long, woody road that stretched for miles on. Cosette sat quietly on the passenger seat, clutching her jacket tensely as she noticed that Crane's driving was becoming erratic, and that sweat beaded and trickled down his forehead. She knew that something was terribly wrong, and she was unsure what to do.

"Are you alright?" Cosette asked quietly.

"Yes, Cosette, I'm fine," Crane replied shakily.

"No, you're not. Why are you frightened?"

"I'm not frightened," Crane retorted.

"It's alright if you are. I'm frightened all the—"

"Hush, Cosette!" Crane barked.

Cosette flinched at his sharp tone and quieted, realizing that she wouldn't be able to calm him down.

They drove for a while more before they got into town.

"Tell me how to get to Carnifex's office."

"He's not going to be there at this hour of the morning," Cosette remarked.

Crane sighed gruffly before hitting the steering wheel. He then pulled out his phone and handed it to her.

"Call him. Tell him to meet us there and nothing else," Crane said.

Cosette took the phone and dialed Dr. Carnifex. It took a moment before the doctor answered.

"Hello, this is Dr. Osiris Carnifex speaking. How may I help you?" came the doctor's mildly confused and groggy voice.

"Doctor, this is Cosette."

"Cosette? Are you alright? Abberline told me you were abducted—"

"Yes, yes, but you must meet us at your office at once."

"Us? Cosette, are you with Crane—?"

"Just meet us there, alright, Doctor?"

"Yes, alright, alright. I'll just take a moment—"

Crane snatched the phone away from her.

"Come alone!" he barked into the phone, before hanging up.

When they got into town, Cosette directed Crane to Dr. Carnifex's office, though no one was there yet when they arrived. This clearly irritated Crane for he slammed the car door roughly and tapped his foot impatiently, huffing every now and then.

"He said he would only take a minute!" Crane exclaimed.

"He'll be here," Cosette assured him.

"He must be getting the police," Crane assumed.

"No, he isn't. He'll come alone; he's just caught up in traffic," the girl remarked.

Crane still wasn't convinced, but soon enough, and to Cosette's relief, Dr. Carnifex's car pulled into the parking lot. He calmly stepped out of his car to greet them.

"Hello, you must be Mr. Draven Crane. Do come inside," Dr. Carnifex offered.

He put his arm around Cosette's shoulders, drawing the key from his pocket and unlocking the door, letting them all inside.

Crane was muttering to himself agitatedly and wringing his hands, seeming to forget himself and his surroundings. The doctor let them into his office and turned on the lights, and directed them to sit down."

"Would you like for Cosette to wait outside—?"

"She stays," Crane snapped briefly.

Dr. Carnifex nodded and motioned for Cosette to sit at his desk. She did so and began to play with the notepad, folding the paper into many origami shapes.

"This is a very unexpected visit, you know, Mr. Crane," Dr. Carnifex said, sitting down in his armchair and picking up his notepad.

Crane only grunted, staring off somewhere in the room.

"Perhaps you could tell me what was the causation of your feeling the need to rush here so suddenly?"

"Is it wrong to protect someone you love?" Crane asked, slowly, without meeting the doctor's eyes.

"No, I would think it was noble," the doctor replied.

"And what of protecting people you don't know?"

"That as well," the doctor agreed, nodding.

"My father wanted to kill Nora," Crane said. "He was going to kill those other women as well."

It was then that Cosette stood from the doctor's desk and went over to him, whispering something into his ear. Crane looked up, scowling.

"What has she said?" he growled suspiciously.

"She has said that your father has been dead for around twenty-two years," Dr. Carnifex related.

Crane looked between the two, almost as if confused.

"He is *not* dead," the man said. "I've seen him."

"Where have you seen him?" the doctor asked.

"When I'm alone. Sometimes when I'm with people, but mostly when I'm alone."

"Does he say anything to you?"

"Yes."

"What does he say?"

"Horrible things. That he'll kill Nora, or me, or—" his eyes wandered to Cosette.

"He speaks to you, is that all?"

"No, he harms me as well."

"Harms you? Is that what happened to your face?"

Crane reached up and touched his bruised, bloody face gingerly.

"Yes. He did this tonight, just before we came here. This is the worst it's ever been."

"Why do you think it was worse this time?" Dr. Carnifex asked.

"Because I fought back," Crane replied.

Dr. Carnifex raised his eyebrows.

"Have you ever fought back against your father before?"

"No."

"Why start now?"

Crane's eyes traveled to Cosette once more.

"He said he was going to kill Cosette."

"And that's why you came to me."

Crane nodded.

"I had to get her away. *I* had to get away. I haven't any idea what to do."

"And you will protect her like the other women?"

"No. I won't kill her."

"So you admit you killed those women?"

Crane stared at his shoes.

"Your father is dead, Mr. Crane."

"No, he isn't!" Crane exclaimed adamantly, leaping out of the chair.

"Perhaps not to you then, but he is nothing more than a fragment of your imagination," Dr. Carnifex remarked.

"That isn't so!" Crane shouted, beginning to pace the floor of the office.

"And why is it not?"

"Because—because that would mean my killing—those women's deaths were pointless! Pointless! I would have been protecting them from nothing more than a nightmare!"

"You experience such guilt," Dr. Carnifex mused. "That you have created your own nightmares so as not to face your own sin. Until you can accept what you have done, and realize that who you are and what you have done are two completely different things, your father will forever have power over you."

"My father has no power over me!" Crane growled, clenching his fists.

"It would seem otherwise," the doctor said. "Tell me, what sort of relationship did you have with your father?"

"I told you, he was an abusive son of a bitch. We didn't have any 'relationship.' He just beat me."

"And did he ever threaten to kill you?"

"He threatened to kill me and take everything I cared for away from me. I tried to rid myself of him for the longest time, but I suppose I can't in the long run."

"You can get rid of him. Don't you know?"

"I can't."

"You can, and you know how?"

"How?"

"Accept that he is dead."

"No!"

"This guilt is your own, and no one else's. You can't keep blaming people for your own actions. One day you will have to face them, let them go, and learn how to live."

"I have to go," Crane muttered suddenly.

"That is very well, but I must implore that Cosette remains with me," Dr. Carnifex said.

"No!" Crane barked. "Cosette, come along."

Cosette, though, didn't move from where she stood at the doctor's desk.

"Cosette, come along at once!" Crane exclaimed.

"I must ask you to go now, sir—"

Crane had clearly grown impatient and withdrew a gun, hidden inside his jacket and pointed it at the doctor.

"We *will* be going now," Crane growled, cocking the gun.

Crane grabbed Cosette by the wrist and pulled her out of the office, walking backwards and never taking his eyes off the doctor.

Dr. Carnifex sighed, frowning as he watched Crane force Cosette into the passenger seat and drive away from the parking lot. He took from his pocket a small recorder quite like the one Pandora Crestmont carried with her, pressed the pause button and set it down on his desk, resting on the desk himself. He then picked up his phone and called Agent Abberline.

"Hello, Doctor?" Abberline answered.

"Crane just visited me for an unpaid session. He had Cosette with him," Dr. Carnifex remarked.

"What? Is he still there?"

"No, he just left."

"How could you just let him leave with Cosette?"

"Perhaps it was the gun he supported?" the doctor replied.

"How long ago did he leave?'

"It hasn't been more than a minute."

"So we haven't much time to set up," Abberline muttered to himself.

"What was that, sir?"

"Cosette called us only a while before they came to see you. We managed to track the call and we're on our way now."

"Tell me where he's going," Dr. Carnifex said.

"No, Doctor, it's not safe for you."

"But—"

"Just let us handle it."

Abberline hung up and Dr. Carnifex sighed again, sitting back in his chair. He picked at the little origami Cosette had made. There was a heart, and some flowers, butterflies, and a cat, but the one that caught his attention was the paper crane she had folded.

Inspecting it closer, he noticed that something was written on it and unfolded it. Inside was the address of the house Cosette was being held in, for she had caught it from the mailbox as the car lights had shone on it. The doctor took up his coat and hurried from the room.

Chapter Twenty-Eight:

Crane was obviously very aggravated by all the doctor had said. Of course, the doctor seemed to have a trick of aggravating people with the truth; he had done as much with herself, though she wasn't a crazed serial killer who might kill because of such words. So, Cosette remained quiet on the way back.

They drove once more into the rural woods, out to where the streetlights disappeared, and only the stars and the moon shone reassuringly in the darkness.

That is, they shone beside the headlights in Crane's driveway.

Cosette sat up straight. There were several cars, a S.W.A.T team van and an ambulance in Crane's driveway, awaiting them.

"Shit," Crane growled and hurried to back out again, but another car only pulled in behind him.

"Cosette get in the backseat and keep your head down in case they start shooting."

The girl followed his instructions but was soon jostled about as Crane sped off the driveway into the dense forest.

There was the sound of cars attempting to follow them,

several shots, one of which went through the back window and out the front, then more shouting.

The car rattled her around so much that she struck her head on the door and grunted in pain. Frowning, she looked up and noticed the lock.

Crane seemed distracted enough so she tried the lock. It clicked open. It would be incredibly risky and dangerous, seeing as how she could easily get hit by the pursuing cars, but she was willing to take that risk.

She waited until there was an opening so that she wouldn't slam into one of the trees, and then she jumped out.

She could hear Crane shout, but it was too late for him to stop and turn back.

Cosette narrowly avoided getting hit by one of the pursuing cars by rolling out of the way. She watched in surprise as the cars drove away. The next moment, someone was pulling her up by the arm.

"Cosette! Cosette, are you alright?" Agent Abberline was asking her.

"Yeah—yeah, I'm okay," Cosette replied, brushing dirt off her skirt and the leaves from her hair.

Abberline bustled about trying to figure out if Crane had been caught or not when Cosette was approached by Dr. Vale.

"Dr. Vale? What are you doing here?" the girl asked, mildly surprised.

"I'm here for you. We're going home," she replied.

There was a while of silence between the two, another car came down the road and pulled into the driveway. Dr. Carnifex jumped out and hurried to where Cosette said in the ambulance.

"Cosette, are you quite alright?" he asked, taking her by the hand.

"Yes, yes, I'm alright, Doctor," the girl answered.

"Doctor, how on earth did you figure out where we were?" Agent Abberline asked in surprise when he spotted Dr. Carnifex.

"Cosette slipped me the address while she was at my office," the doctor answered, nodding at the girl.

"I saw it on the mailbox on our way to the doctor's," Cosette added.

"I'm glad you did, or we might never have found you," Abberline remarked. "But Crane is still out there. We're going to have you stay in a safe house with Dr. Vale until further notice."

"I can look after myself, thank you," Cosette remarked.

"I've no doubt you can, but I'd rather you be somewhere safe in case Crane shows back up again."

"He kidnapped me from her house. Who's to say he won't try again?"

"We'll have officers patrol the street for tonight, and then we'll get you somewhere safe, don't worry."

Cosette had wanted to see how the chase would play out, but she wasn't reluctant to leave either. With Abberline's promise to relate all that had happened the next time he saw her, she went away, escorted by Dr. Vale.

It was quiet as they rode, except for the gentle music that played on the radio.

"Are you alright?" Vale asked her, breaking the silence.

"Yes," Cosette replied.

"Are you sure?"

"Yes, why?"

"You don't seem too distressed."

"Should I?"

"Considering what you just experienced, I'd say so."

"Oh," Cosette said. "Well, I'm fine."

When they arrived at Dr. Vale's house, Cosette was very tired indeed, but felt utterly disgusted by the dirt from her event and showered before going to bed, lulled to sleep by the purr of the police cars driving up and down the street.

When she woke in the morning, she was greeted by Dr. Vale, who had taken over the kitchen and was preparing fried eggs and bacon in a pan. There were also some muffins sitting on a plate on the counter.

After breakfast the phone began to ring. Cosette picked up when she saw it was Agent Abberline.

"Hey, did you get him?" the girl asked hopefully.

"No, he managed to evade us. He caused a car wreck in order to get away, but everyone's okay. We're going to have to move you to one of our apartments, though."

"Like a safehouse?" Cosette asked.

"Yeah, basically," Abberline said.

"Cool," the girl replied.

"I'll send Creed by to pick you up. We've already got a place set up for you," Agent Abberline said. "So be ready when he gets there. It should be around two."

Cosette had packed her things and put Magnolia in her carrier by the time Det. Creed arrived. He knocked on the door looking extremely tired. He exchanged greetings with the doctor before they left the house, parting ways. Det. Creed drove to another very nice apartment complex, and they went inside.

There were security cameras and several guards disguised as residents about the place. The head-detective took Cosette up to one of the apartments.

Cosette was taking it all in, thinking that it would make for a lovely experience to apply to her novels.

"So, is this place like the safehouses in James Bond?" Cosette asked.

"Yeah, this place has security cameras, motion sensors, microphones, guards all in case Crane tries to show up again," Det. Creed replied.

He consumed several more cups of coffee in the few hours he was to stay with Cosette and make sure she was alright before Det. Everglow showed up to relieve him of his post.

"Hi, Cosette," Everglow greeted her. "How are you?"

"I'm fine," the girl replied. "This is all very interesting, isn't it?"

"I suppose you could look at it that way," Everglow agreed.

"I've gotten quite a bit of writing done. I missed my deadline for the newspaper, but I'm sure they won't mind once they hear what's happened."

"You know, Cosette, I'm terribly sorry about getting you

involved with our plan to lure out Crane," Everglow apologized.

"It isn't your fault," Cosette replied. "If it's anyone's fault, it's Pandora Crestmont's."

Everglow laughed.

"I do hope Pandora gets fired though," Cosette remarked.

"Me too, though I'm not sure they'll let her go. This isn't the first time she's done something that could technically be considered illegal. The paper runs on her stories and, therefore, her dishonest nature. That's why the Exposeé is so popular."

Cosette chuckled.

"I thought that Crane would surely try to kill you after reading the article. I was terribly worried for you actually. Who would have thought that he would have gone after me because my name was mentioned in the article? Well, then again, I suppose I should have expected it. Though I do think he meant to kidnap me anyways."

"What do you mean?" Det. Everglow asked.

"Well, that was a bit of a plot twist. You know how he was my neighbor? Well, when I left him that welcome basket, I think he became frankly obsessed. I feel badly. He hasn't experienced much kindness, has he? But when he kidnapped me, he kept talking about how I would have been his and Nora's daughter if she had lived. It was terribly nonsensical."

"He really must be insane," Everglow remarked, shaking her head.

"Yes, well, guilt can do that to a person. Just think of *A Tell-Tale Heart*. I do think he needs help, and that he *can* be helped, and one day he'll be able to come to terms with himself."

"But don't you feel just the slightest resentment towards him for what he did to you?"

"Not really. He's made this story very intriguing," Cosette replied.

Det. Everglow looked sideways at her.

"Yes," the girl continued. "And when he gets caught, I do hope it makes for a good ending. And I hope they catch him soon. I'd like to get this novel out."

"Cosette, you *do* realize all this happened *to you* in *real life,* don't you?" Everglow asked.

"Yes. Why wouldn't I?"

"You just don't seem terribly affected by it."

"Well, I don't feel very affected."

Chapter Twenty-Nine:

Cosette didn't quite mind that she couldn't go out seeing as how she didn't go out much anyways. She liked this apartment much better than her own, as it was larger and didn't smell like must.

Abberline came to visit her once, and she told him all that had happened when Crane had kidnapped her. Everglow and Seymour had visited a few times as well. As had Creed (on "strictly business" as he said.) The rest of the time, the guards were unknown officials.

She spent most of her time reading, watching the television, working on the cover art for her book, and most of all, writing.

Abberline had scheduled her another appointment with Dr. Carnifex, who she was supposed to visit, but Judith had called to say that the doctor had unfortunately had to cancel all his appointments due to an emergency with another patient. Cosette hoped that Gustav hadn't tried to jump off a bridge or something. With the cancellation of her session, Cosette returned to the safehouse and turned on the television for background noise while she wrote.

The situation had been explained to Mr. Bedford, Cosette's editor-in-chief, and he said she didn't have to write anything else for the paper until her ordeal was over. Of course, Cosette had continued to write and send in her stories to be published anyways.

She had been working on her novel for about three hours and was becoming more involved in the television show rather than her novel when she smelled something strange. It smelled like smoke. Someone on the floor must have lit a cigarette, she supposed.

Within a few moments, though, the smell grew stronger. She was just thinking of going to ask at the front desk to have whoever was smoking to put out their cigarette when the fire alarms began to blare and the sprinklers activated.

One of the guards hurried in.

"There's a fire downstairs and it's spreading quickly. We've got to evacuate," he said calmly.

Cosette hurried and grabbed her duffle bags, which she had luckily not unpacked and followed the official downstairs to the lobby. She saw that there was in fact a rapidly spreading fire that had started in the club house and spread to one of the conference rooms. They stood outside and soon the fire was spilling out the front doors and catching the second floor. It seemed to be spreading abnormally fast as well, almost as if it had been set. And she was right.

The Abberlines had arrived with the fire trucks, ambulances and police cars and when the fire had been put out, Agent Abberline approached Cosette, who had been watching the spectacle, holding her luggage and cat.

"Cosette, I'm having Dr. Vale come pick you up," he said to her.

"Why? I can just walk to my apartment."

"You're not going back to your apartment."

"Why not?"

"It's still a crime scene and..." he sighed heavily. "Look, kid, I don't think it's safe for you to live on your own."

"What?" she exclaimed.

"You aren't stable enough to live alone," Abberline admitted.

Cosette scowled at him, looking offended.

"I don't want to have to put you in the system. Just stay with Dr. Vale for a little bit. It's not forever, and I'm not asking you to sell your apartment or anything."

Cosette didn't answer.

Chapter Thirty:

She had been reading in her room when her phone began to ring. It was Seymour.

She picked up.

"Cosette, you have to come down to the apartment complex that you stayed in."

"I thought it caught fire," Cosette said.

"It did. But you've got to come if you want the end of your novel."

"You caught Crane?"

"Sort of. Just come."

When he had hung up, Cosette grabbed her purse and hurried out of the house without any disturbance seeing as how Vale was gone teaching classes.

She evaded the police cars on duty and caught a cab to the apartment complex. The whole station seemed to be there. She saw Agent Abberline and tried to slip by him to get into the complex, but the man spotted her.

"Cosette, what are you doing here?" he asked.

"I heard something was going on over here. Possibly connected with my story," the girl replied.

"Well, we haven't gone in yet. We only have what we hear over the call sent by the building inspector."

"What did they say?"

"The inspector had come to look around after the fire when he found a body."

"A body?" Cosette repeated. "Whose?"

"Supposedly Crane's."

"What?" Cosette exclaimed. "So what are you waiting for then? Let's go in!"

"Hold on. By the description the inspector gave, it might disturb you greatly."

"I've got to see it for my book."

"Always for your books," Abberline muttered. "Fine, but, I go in first to see the crime scene."

Cosette agreed to this, and she waited outside while Dets. Creed, Everglow, Knox, the Abberlines, and the forensics team went inside.

After a while, Cosette got impatient and decided to go inside to see for herself what they had found. She found the detectives, the director, and the Mortensens inspecting the crime scene, which lay out in the living room and made Cosette stop in her tracks, her eyes widening at the sight before her.

Crane was dead.

His corpse sat on the sofa, empty eyes staring forward. His mouth was half open and stained with blood. His ring finger had been cut off, his wedding ring still on it, and was held by his other hand, which rested in his lap. His throat had been cut and he had been stabbed through the heart with a hunting knife, which pinned a piece of paper to the corpse. Ladybug Mortensen carefully removed the knife and handed the paper over to Det. Creed to examine.

"Hey, look at this," he said after inspecting it.

They crowded around to read the note. It read:

One for Sorrow
Two for Mirth
Three for a Death
Four for a Birth
Five for Silver
Six for Gold

Seven for a Secret Never to be Told
Eight for a Promise
Nine is Forsworn
Ten is a Treasure Hidden 'Neath Thorn
Eleven Brings Storm
Twelve Shall be Fair
Thirteen Cruel Whisper
Fourteen a Care
Fifteen a Sojourn
Sixteen for Home
Seventeen Finds You Standing Alone
Eighteen is Good Fortune
Nineteen Justice Done
Twenty the First Sign an End Has Begun

The first verse was scratched out in red ink.

"This is an old poem from the eighteenth century," Det. Everglow remarked.

"And a major clue," Cosette said. "There was a superstition in that time period that the amount of crows you counted would tell you what your future held."

"But what does it mean?" Det. Knox asked.

"It means that whoever killed Crane killed him out of grief and revenge. They were Crane's enemy. He did something to hurt them," Cosette remarked.

"Oh, yeah, that narrows it down a lot. The man probably had tons of enemies," Det. Creed said.

"But it narrows it down more," the chief replied.

The detectives continued their investigation. Cosette, though, couldn't help but sit and stare at Crane's dead body.

"Why do you look mopey?" Det. Creed asked, sitting down on the coffee table beside her. "Your kidnapper's dead, you can go home, and finish your godforsaken book that we never hear the end of."

"It's hardly the end of my story. I'm sure it will go on long after this. But I can't help but feel pity for Crane," Cosette said. "Maybe if he had lived, he might have been able to change."

“Look, kid, maybe he could’ve changed, maybe he couldn’t have. But it doesn’t matter. He's dead now.”

“I don’t think he knew what he was doing was wrong,” Cosette said.

“Sometimes the greatest evil is thinking you’re doing something good when in actuality, you’re doing something terrible,” Creed said.

Cosette nodded ponderously for a moment.

“That’s good actually. I think I’ll put that in my novel,” she remarked.

“All you think about is that book,” Det. Creed groaned, shaking his head as he stood up and went away.

❀❀❀

Agent Abberline had forensics to analyze the corpse. He, his wife, and the detectives went to oversee the operation, and, of course, Cosette had brought herself along.

“So,” Mortensen said, when the operations were done. “There are no fingerprints on the corpse or on the weapon, and no other form of DNA anywhere.”

“So this was planned,” Det. Creed said.

“And seemingly by someone who knows what they’re doing,” Det. Everglow added.

“We did find one clue, though,” Mortensen remarked.

“What is it?” the chief asked.

Mortensen held up a finger for them to wait and went to retrieve an evidence bag. He handed it over to them and they saw that it was a black origami crane, stained with blood.

“We found this in his throat,” Mortensen said.

“Just like Herrod,” Creed connected.

“This is justice,” Cosette remarked. “Justice for the killer’s sorrow. And this isn’t a paper crane. It’s a paper crow. ‘One for Sorrow.’ Our killer is counting crows.”

www.ingramcontent.com/pod-product-compliance
Lightning Source LLC
LaVergne TN
LVHW090606110826
845146LV00001B/275

* 9 7 9 8 9 9 3 9 0 4 4 0 5 *